ssles, Heart-Pings! and
ad, Happy Endings...

I no   l something: without even realizing what
he w   loing, Billy's hand had stopped whirling his
base   cap around in that demented way and was
now   iveying a Jaffa Cake to his mouth.

"N   n! These are just ace, aren't they?" he
mur   ed after a mouthful, looking slightly less
defl   ! all of a sudden.

H   it wasn't earth-shattering stuff, but it
seen   like a positive sign to me. Billy would be all
righ   I, Ally Love, his best mate, would make
sure   it. And if Jaffa Cakes helped him over his
orde   then how much better would he be if there
was   otential new girlfriend on the scene?

    then the spookiest thing happened — I
ca   Billy sort of staring at me as if he could
re   y thoughts. But nah; that rapturous look was
pro   ly (definitely) nothing to do with Billy
su   ly developing amazing psychic powers and
e   ything to do with the joy of Jaffa Cakes...

To find out more about Karen McCombie,
visit her website www.karenmccombie.com

ALLY'S WORLD

KAREN McCOMBIE

HASSLES, HEART-PINGS! and SAD, HAPPY ENDINGS...

SCHOLASTIC

FOR
(who w   It to)

First p   oks
An imprint of Scholastic Ltd
Euston House, 24 Eversholt Street
London, NW1 1DB, UK
Registered office: Westfield Road, Southam, Warwickshire, CV47 0RA
SCHOLASTIC and associated logos are trademarks and or registered
trademarks of Scholastic Inc.

This edition published by Scholastic Ltd, 2007

10 digit ISBN 0 439 94348 5
13 digit ISBN 978 0439 94348 2

British Library Cataloguing-in-Publication Data.
A CIP catalogue record for this book is available from the British Library

Printed by Bookmarque Ltd, Croydon, Surrey
Papers used by Scholastic Children's Books are made from wood grown in
sustainable forests.

3 5 7 9 10 8 6 4 2

www.scholastic.co.uk/zone

Contents

PROLOGUE

Dear Mum,

I, Ally Love, am going mad. Honest.

I've just been staring out my window, looking at Alexandra Palace perched on the hill, and you know what I thought? I thought the sky looked *exactly* like the opening credits of *The Simpsons* – you know, when the fat, fluffy white clouds separate and show the titles. I kind of half expected to see the words "The Love Family" floating above Ally Pally.

See? Told you I was going mad. But *happily* mad, you'll be pleased to hear...

Actually, talking about *The Simpsons*, you know the guy who invented them? Matt Groaning or Groening or something? Well, apart from being a genius (for inventing *The Simpsons*, natch), did you know he also drew cartoons? I used to have a photocopy of one cartoon he did*, called "The 24 Warning Signs of Stress". It was very funny (and perfect for an undercover worrier like me). For one of the signs of stress, there was this drawing of a guy with a twisty head – all eyes, ears and nose in a tangle – and that kind of sums up how *I* feel when I've got a head full of hassles.

And there were loads of worrisome hassles – as well as weird heart-pings! – going on recently, weren't there? In fact, there were *so* many that it's taken *extra* long for me to write everything down 'cause it's taken *extra* long for my head to untangle.

But I have finally scribbled it all here, and stuff makes more sense now that I've done that – the stuff to do with Linn, of course, but all the stuff with Sandie and Billy in particular. Hey, maybe, *just* this once, I'll show my journal to someone else apart from you … but then I don't know if reading about everything would make Sandie sad again, when she's sounding so happy (I spoke to her on the phone half an hour ago and she wouldn't shut up about how gorgeous her room is now she's painted it lilac and lime – eek!).

Maybe I should let Billy have a nosey at it? Nope, no, no *way* – that's *never* going to happen. He's such a berk that if I let him read it and then asked him what he thought about it, he'd probably burp the national anthem or start talking like Cartman out of *South Park* or something just to hide his embarrassment. And then that would make me annoyed (and embarrassed).

So ... it's for your eyes only, Mum. A record of all the hassles, the heart-pings! and the rest. At least I can trust you not to go wibbly on me or act like a hyperactive baboon, like certain people I could mention...

Love you lots,
Ally
(your happily mad Love Child No. 3)

* I think Winslet ate it – doh!

Chapter 1

THE WELCOME BACK DOOR PARTY

I had a shadow. It followed me everywhere: to the park, to the shops, to my room.

The other day, it even tried to follow me to the loo, till I told it (nicely) to get lost and slammed the door in its face.

My shadow had a name, and that was Billy.

Oh, yes. Ever since Sandie dumped him the week before – right after our geography field trip – Billy had hung around my house (and me) like a stray puppy with a face like a wet sock. I guess it was understandable; when you're mooching, pining and miserable, the one person you turn to is your best mate, isn't it? I mean, Billy has other friends, but they're boys, and let's face it, boys are not too great at doling out sympathy. Well, maybe they are when you've missed a dead cert goal during a five-a-side game in the park, or you dropped your GameBoy and it won't start up or something. But if you're a lad who's just been humiliatingly dumped by your girlfriend, the closest you're going to get to sympathy from another lad is a mumbled "Oh…" followed by a rude joke about the size of your ex's nose/bum/knees to cheer you up.

So you can't blame Billy for turning to me instead of Stevie or Hassan in his moment of need. The trouble was, it wasn't just a moment; it had been a whole, full-on six days now. Yep, Billy was shadowing me around, desperate for my advice/pity/company practically every minute I wasn't asleep or in school (or in the loo). I guess it was 'cause, unlike Hassan and Stevie, I seemed to know the exact right things to say…

- "Mmm … yeah … definitely… I know…" (Rule no. 1 when you're sympathizing with people: agree with just about everything they say.)

- "OK, so you feel like poo right now, but you won't for ever." (Rule no. 2: remind them that things will get better, even if you're not sure that's true.)

- "No – just 'cause Sandie chucked you, it *doesn't* mean you're a total, no-hope loser dork." (Rule no. 3: try to boost their flattened ego.)

- "Do you want more ice-cream/nachos/another HobNob?" (Rule no. 4: offer comfort food – vats of it. In times of trauma, some people might not be able to face food, but, miraculously, Billy was still managing to stuff his face very nicely thank you in-between whingeing.)

So, now it was Saturday, and we had a week's worth of half-term break looming in front of us. Which meant, I supposed, that Billy would be doing his limpet act and sticking to me for even *more* hours of the day. I wouldn't have minded, honest I wouldn't (considering the circumstances), but the big problem was … well … *Sandie*.

It's your worst nightmare when two friends start going out with each other, isn't it? What I mean is, the knowledge that one day they'll break up and not be able to *stand* being within a ten kilometre radius of each other. And that's what had happened with Billy and Sandie. Billy – with his heart well and truly trampolined on and his self-confidence squashed like a mushy pea – wasn't exactly in the mood to hang out with Sandie any time soon (like any time this *century*). And Sandie – never exactly the bravest girl in the world in the first place – felt so hideously hideous about finishing with Billy that the very thought of bumping into him made her feel like she might *hurl*.

It was basically one big drag that we couldn't all just hang out together as usual during the holiday, either just us three or with Kyra or Chloe or the others. So I decided I had to do *something*. I had to somehow *force* them to meet up, just so they could get over the hurdle of facing each other for the first time, and then *maybe* they would be cool with each other after that. Well, cool*ish*. At least so they could maybe face being in the same room together without fainting. (That would be a *start*.)

But how was I going to do it? Two hours ago, I wouldn't have had the feeblest clue. But then a couple of things happened that made an idea ping like an oasis into the barren emptiness of my brain. First up, Dad called from his bike shop and told me that he'd got the right hinges and was finally, *finally* planning on re-hanging my bedroom door this afternoon. Oh, the joy of having a door to close instead of a gaping wide *nothing* between me and my mad family! Now I could dance around the room in my knickers and wellies or juggle cacti nude and no one would know. (Er, not that I *particularly* wanted to dance around in my knickers and wellies or juggle cacti nude; it's just that it would be nice to have the choice.)

Anyway, Dad and the door was Thing 1 that got me thinking. Thing 2 was Mum's batty idea to celebrate the momentous occasion of me having a door once more.

"*I* know!" she'd beamed, when me and Billy

were helping her clear away the dishes after lunch. "We should have a Welcome Back Door Party! We can make streamers and a banner and everything! What do you think, Ally?"

What I'd thought was, *Fine … anything to give me a break from talking about The Big Split with Billy for the thirty millionth time.*

"Sure!" I'd nodded, before Tor and Ivy went into party hyperdrive and started babbling about party hats and cake.

Mum was just getting as hyper as they were and talking about whether we should make a cake or just have loads and loads of Maltesers instead, when The Idea clattered into my mind: why didn't I phone Sandie and invite her round to join in the silliness? (Er, without mentioning the fact that Billy was here, of course.) The way I saw it, how could you hold on to grudges or guilt during something as completely dumb as a Welcome Back Door Party?

So, I sneaked off and called her, and she said yes, please, and she'd be here before five. Ten out of ten for my ace plan so far. The only problem now was that it was a bit past five o'clock, and there was no sign of Sandie. I was too twitchy to concentrate on the newspaper hats that Mum was showing us how to make in the living room; it was time to make another sneaky phone call and see what she was up to.

"Back in a minute!" I said vaguely in the direction of anyone who might be listening (i.e. Mum, Billy, Tor, Ivy, assorted pets, and Rowan too).

Before I dived out of the door, I plonked my version of a paper hat on to the coffee table. What a disaster it was – not so much origami as just a scrunched-up bit of newspaper. Even Billy, in the depths of gloom, was making a better job of the party hat thing than I was.

"Hello?"

To be honest, I was kind of surprised to hear Sandie's voice. I guess I'd been expecting her mum or dad, and was supposing they'd say that she'd left ten minutes ago and would be ringing my doorbell any second now.

"Why are you there? Aren't you supposed to be *here*?" I asked bluntly.

"Er … 'cause I'm not coming?" Sandie answered nervously.

"Huh? What do you mean, you're not coming? What about the Welcome Back Door Party? We're making hats and having Maltesers and everything!"

"I know. And I really want to come."

"So … why don't you come?"

There was an ominous silence from Sandie. And then there wasn't. "'Cause Billy's there, right?"

Urgh, she'd sussed me out. I was about as transparent as one of those spooky jellyfish that Tor likes gawping at in the Web Of Life at London Zoo.

"Yeah, but…"

Pathetic. I couldn't think of anything to say after "but".

"I just don't want to see him, Ally! Not yet! I still feel like a total creep for chucking him!"

Then I felt bad for Sandie and seriously mean for trying to trick her into coming. I guess I'd have felt as sick as someone on a North Sea ferry in a blizzard if someone had fixed me up to spend time in a confined space with Keith Brownlow or Feargal O'Leary straight after we'd finished. Not that I even got *started* with either of them; it was hardly all lovey-doveyness and cutesy pet names with me and Keith, never mind me and Feargal. Not like Sandie and her "Baby Bear". (Blee – don't remind me, or I really *will* barf…)

"OK. Sorry. Whatever…" I mumbled, feeling like a total louse. "But how did you know?"

"'Cause after I got off the phone earlier, it dawned on me that you'd been kind of whispering. But I wasn't *sure* he was there. Till now."

"How come?" I found myself frowning, though no one could see that except for Colin, who was snoozling directly in my eyeline on a carpeted step halfway up the stairs. (Er, except he'd have needed to open his eyes first to clock me.)

"Because you're whispering *now*," said Sandie.

Doh...

My frazzled brain was frantically scrabbling around for something to say that would make things right when Sandie jumped right in and spoke again.

"Anyway, I've got some brilliant news!" she enthused, sounding instantly brighter.

Speaking of instantly brighter, the front door suddenly burst open and Dad and Linn came in chattering, along with an accompaniment of frantic, thrilled barking from Winslet, Rolf and Ben.

"Like?" I asked Sandie, not bothering to whisper now that the chattering, barking and yelling (that was Tor and Ivy) was acting as cover for my conversation.

"Like..." she paused, for maximum impact, "...like Jacob is coming to London on Wednesday!"

I knew she wanted me to say stuff like "Wow!" and "Yay!" and "That's so cool!" But no matter how great it was for Sandie to see her new boyfriend – the lad she'd met on our geography field trip – I just couldn't do the whole wow, yay, that's-so-cool thing when I'd had one soggy, sad boy to prop up all week.

"That's nice," was about as enthusiastic as I could manage.

While I was still on the phone, I gave Dad a quick grin and a nod as he zoomed by me straight up the stairs, holding his toolbox aloft in one hand and giving me a thumbs-up with the other. And following behind him, giggling and yakking, were my whole family (including dogs and a bemused Billy), stomping after Dad like he was the Pied Piper or something. (Colin had to wake up and bound out of the way pretty smartish – not that easy when you've only got three legs.)

"Yeah, I know!" gushed Sandie. "And I can't wait to see him again!"

Hmm … *not* all of my family had giggled and yakked their way up the stairs with their home-made party hats and bags of Maltesers; Ivy was by my side, earnestly gazing up at me as she tugged at the bottom of my T-shirt, muttering, "C'mon, Ally – part*eeeeee*!"

"OK, Ivy," I nodded down at her. "You go on up – I'll be there in a second! Sorry, Sandie, but I'd better go. I think they're starting the Door Party without me."

Ivy allowed herself to be shooed upstairs, smiling broadly at me through the bannister and showing off all her cute baby teeth. Somewhere above me up on the top floor – where my attic bedroom shared space with Linn's – the sound of creaking floorboards and laughter drifted down.

"Oh, right," said Sandie. "But hold on – I just remembered. Do you want to come to tea tomorrow night? Mum asked me to ask you specially."

Of course I said yes, even though meals round at Sandie's are always on the bleurgh side (her mum likes to boil everything till you end up with something that looks like a pile of wallpaper paste when she finally plonks it on your plate). And it would be nice to catch up with Sandie, even though I wasn't sure how I was going to get out of my permanent babysitting duties with Billy.

So we set a time, and said our byes, but it wasn't till I was bounding up the stairs two at a time to join the celebrations that something weird struck me (not literally – I don't mean a leaping salmon *pounced* out of the shadows and slapped me in the face or anything). It was just the fact that Sandie's mum had asked me to tea, *specially*?! She *never* did that! Sure I stayed for meals sometimes, but that was usually 'cause I was already there doing homework or whatever and Sandie asked me to.

The thing is, with both Sandie's super-straight parents I always got the feeling that they kind of just *put up* with me being Sandie's friend. I mean, Mr and Mrs Walker are really, *really* uptight and protective of Sandie, and I'm sure they think I'm this wild, rebellious girl, all because my family is a bit disorganized. (Well, I guess we *did* manage to lose our mum for four years...)

But whatever. I'd just have to figure out a way to shake off my shadow (called Billy) for one evening without hurting his black and blue feelings. And I'd worry about that later – I had some serious silliness to be getting on with right now...

"Hurry up, Ally!" Rowan called down to me, leaning over the attic bannister and looking like a pretty version of the Medusa with her bundle of different-sized short plaits dangling around her face. "Dad's just about to put in the final screw!"

I bounded up in time to see everyone wearing their wonky paper hats – including Billy (his was plonked on *top* of his baseball cap), Rolf and Ben (Winslet was ferociously ripping hers to bits).

"There you go!" Mum smiled, sticking the biggest newspaper work-of-art on my head, while Tor held out a bowl of Maltesers to me.

"Nearly there! How does it look, Ally Pally?"

Dad asked me, managing to talk almost normally, despite the screw he was holding between his teeth.

"It looks great!" I nodded in reply, though I wasn't just talking about my long-lost door, but about the brilliant *"Welcome back, Ally's door!"* sign that Rowan had painted in something luminous, and the arch of balloons that Mum had pinned up (they said *"Congratulations – it's a boy!"* on them, but Mum said that's all they had left in the corner shop).

"Here – everyone take one of these. I found them at the back of a drawer in the kitchen!" said Mum, chucking everyone a party popper. "Once that last screw is in, it's blast-off time!"

I shot a quick look at Billy, who had a confused smile stuck on his face, like a toddler that's gone to sleep in their buggy in the park and woken up in a queue in Tesco's and isn't sure how that might have happened.

"OK ... here we ... go!" Dad called out, followed by mass whooping and popping from all of us.

Course the whole thing set the dogs off, and seemed to get Ivy into a happy party muddle; apart from stomping her tiny feet up and down she started singing "Happy birdie to yooooo..." directly to Tor.

"No, babes!" Linn laughed, leaning down and

scooping Ivy up in her arms. "Tor's not eight till *next* Saturday!"

"'Nother party! More 'tesers!" she clapped ecstatically, before shoving a melted ball of chocolate in her mouth.

So, my Welcome Home Door Party had been a success. Everyone was smiling, even Billy (even if his head was on another planet).

But lurking in some dusty dark corner of my brain, a small voice whispered, "Something's weird..." Although that small voice very unhelpfully didn't explain what *exactly* was weird. Was it the fact that poor Billy was still so out of sorts? (He was trying so hard to have fun but pretty much failing.) Was it 'cause I couldn't shake this niggle of annoyance with Sandie ducking out of meeting up with him today? Then again, was it maybe because my perfecto, neat-freak sister Linn was having a great time, and didn't seem to mind the fact that her home-made hat was leaving a newsprint headline on her forehead and that Ivy had just wiped her chocolatey fingers on our big sis's spotless white top? (Linn acting so unconcerned by mess – now that *was* weird.) Or was it just because Ben the golden retriever really, *really* suited his newspaper trilby?

Who knew? But why worry about weirdness

when you've got a mountain of Maltesers to eat? I could figure it out later, in the privacy of my room, with the door firmly closed (i.e. when I was doing my nudey cacti juggling)...

Chapter 2

LOVE AND DROOL...

What a swizz.

For the first time in ages, I had peace, quiet, no Billy and a door. And the swizz was, I felt kind of lonely and bored. Where was my shadow when I needed him? And I didn't have a single snorey cat or dog to keep me company in my bedroom on this dull, restless, sleepless night.

It was nearly twelve o'clock, and Saturday night was about to slink darkly into Sunday morning. I'd gone to bed early, hoping to slip into this pretty cool recurring dream I'd been having lately, where I'm teetering *right* on the verge of (eek!) snogging someone. It was the weirdest thing; every time I dreamt the dream, I'd get this electrifying tummy tingle, knowing I was about to be kissed, but then I'd always wake up before the kiss happened (boo!), and I never got to see who I was not-quite-but-almost kissing either. (Could it be Alfie? Oh, please, oh, please, oh, please ... after all, it would be the only chance I'd get to kiss Linn's best mate/Rowan's boyfriend, sadly.)

But after a couple of hours of tossing, turning and not sleeping – never mind dreaming – I gave up and found myself staring out of my bedroom window at the sight of Alexandra Palace all lit up with floodlights and looking much, *much* grander than it does close up (it's actually kind of crumbly when you're right beside it). The reason it was all floodlit like that was 'cause there was some telly programme being filmed up there. They'd been hovering around Crouch End for a few days now: Rowan had spotted them at the tennis courts beside Highgate Woods on Thursday; Mum had seen them yesterday at a house two doors down from the nursery Ivy had just started going to; and Linn caught a glimpse of them filming at the fish 'n' chip shop on Park Road earlier tonight (dead glam, huh?).

Now, maybe it seems weird that I wasn't coming over all wow!, gosh!, whee! about the idea of a film crew shooting in the neighbourhood, but honestly, it's practically *normal* to see film crews around Crouch End. Location vans and cameras pop up around the corner all the time – producers and location scouts or whoever treat Crouch End like it's an open-air film studio, for some reason. But don't go thinking that the Clocktower on the Broadway is going to be starring in the next Tom Hanks movie, or that snoot director James Cameron is checking out the local pet shop as a possible setting for the next sequel to horror movie *Aliens*. All the filming that's done tends to star no one particularly famous, and is for stuff like a TV documentary about the work of health and safety officers in our area (fun, if you're interested in cockroaches, rats and rising damp). The only time it got vaguely exciting round here was a few years ago when me and Rowan saw some of the cast of *EastEnders* outside the old Town Hall, 'cause they were filming a wedding in there. But even *that* wasn't too exciting, because half the cast of *EastEnders* lives roundabout Ally Pally anyway. (And trust me, they don't look much like celebrities when they're buying beansprouts in the health food shop or fingering dental floss in Boots.)

Actually, the only person I knew who was getting their knickers in a star-struck twist about the whole filming thing was Kyra. (Well, she *was* still newish to Crouch End, I s'pose.) "But it's a TV crew, Ally! What if I could get a walk-on part or something? I could get spotted and be famous!" she'd said to me yesterday, when Jen had told us about spying some filming going on in the scuzzy car park behind Woolworth's. Yeah, of *course* Kyra could get spotted and become famous. *Or* she could get chucked off the set by a security man and told to get lost...

Anyway, enough of Kyra and camera crews and kissing dreams without any kissing (grr...); I was feeling a bit troubled, if you want to know the truth. And the trouble was that I had *two* troubles. The first was that I *still* couldn't shake the weird weirdness from my head, and no matter *how* much I ping-ponged thoughts around in my head, I still couldn't figure out what was bugging me.

The second trouble was, my door worked too well now. I didn't want some new, improved door that shut properly and stayed shut; I wanted a door like the old one; one that would swing open when Colin, or the cats that weren't Colin, or the dogs, or Tor and one of his huge collection of soft toys leant a paw against it.

In fact, right then, I found myself padding across the floor and yanking the door open, in case there was an ark's worth of traumatized pets queueing up on the third-floor landing, wondering why they weren't being allowed to come and drape themselves in purring, snorey bundles around my room.

And so I opened the door, and there, waiting patiently, was no one at all. There was only one thing for it. If they weren't going to come to *me*, I'd go downstairs and grab the first pet I could and drag it up here. Well, grabbing Winslet might not be a great idea. She's not too hot at surprises (unless they're edible). She'd probably surprise me back by sinking her teeth into the nearest bit of me.

Mum was crying.

I wasn't – I was helping myself to my sixth HobNob.

Dad wasn't crying either, mainly 'cause he was slumped fast asleep on one of the armchairs with a cat that wasn't Colin clumsily perched in the nape of his neck, purring and padding its claws into his head.

"*Parrrpppp!*"

That was Mum, blowing her nose on one of the bits of kitchen roll that had been scrunched on the tray in her lap. She'd been trying to make Tor's birthday card (inspired by Ivy getting the song wrong today, she'd spelt out "Happy Birdie, Tor!" in feathers) and that bit of kitchen roll she was parping her nose on probably had some glue on it.

"So, is it a good film, then?" I asked, crunching my biscuit as the sad music swamped the credits.

When I'd come downstairs I found that Mum was staying up late to watch some old 1960s movie called *Dr Zhivago*. She'd said it was a classic romance set during the Russian Revolution, but I think I'd come in too late to see much of the romance bit. All I caught was a bit of Russia looking very snowy and cold, and then the hero as an old man, having a heart attack when he spotted the girl he'd lost years ago (clumsy him). But I didn't mind – it was just nice and cosy to be curled up on the sofa with Mum and biscuits (and Dad, of course, sort of).

"Ooh, yeah ... it's a brilliant love story. All very tragic, though," she smiled at me through watery eyes. She had a tiny bit of feather stuck to the tip of her nose, I noticed, but I didn't say anything. It looked kind of cute.

"A tragic love story ... like Billy and Sandie's?" I said, with a sly grin.

"Exactly like that," Mum grinned back at me. "You've just got to imagine Crouch End as Moscow..."

We both giggled so much that a HobNob crumb went down the wrong way and I got the hiccups and had to drink my glass of milk upside down.

"Poor Billy," sighed Mum, while I was still upside down. "I mean, it was definitely the right thing for Sandie to finish with him, if she fancied someone else. It was much kinder than stringing him along and not telling him. That would have hurt a lot more. But he's not taking it too well, is he?"

I wanted to shake my head, but since I was still sipping milk the wrong way round I was worried I might drown.

"It's tough when it's your first love, I guess," she carried on, the tiny bit of feather rising and falling as the words drifted out of her mouth. "That first time, it hurts so badly that you can't imagine that you'll fall in love again. But you do. And he will."

Even from my upside-down position, I could see Mum was gazing all adoringly at Dad, who'd managed to sleep all through the fancy film music, our giggles and my stupid hiccups.

"Well, I hope Billy falls wham-blam in love soon," I said, slowly turning the right way up and wobbling slightly with a case of the dizzies. "Don't know if I can keep saying all the same things to him over and over again!"

Never mind me overusing all my best sympathy lines on Billy – our family was in danger of starving if he kept up with the comfort eating when he was round our place. (And if he kept up his current munchy ratio, he'd look less like the tall, gangly Billy I knew and loved, and look more like that huge opera bloke Pavarotti. In a baseball cap.)

"Still, you do seem to be saying all the right things to him, even if you *are* having to say them over and over again," Mum smiled, patting my hand. "But anyway, I wouldn't look for Billy falling wham-blam in love with anyone soon. He's got to give himself moping time."

"Moping time? Is that a proper thing? A proper term, I mean?"

"Absolutely," Mum answered, but smiling and shaking her head to let me know she'd made it up. (This was fun. I was so glad Mum had decided to come back home and live with us again.)

"But anyway..." she carried on, putting the feathery tray on the coffee table and curling her legs up underneath her on the sofa, like one of the cats (only in a hippy, Indian skirt). "That thing you said about falling in love wham-blam – it doesn't really happen like that."

"Doesn't it?" I frowned. I had absolutely no idea. OK, so I had a planet-sized crush on Alfie, and I'd tried to talk myself into liking Keith Brownlow and Feargal O'Leary when I found out *they* liked *me* (it didn't work either time), but I'd never been *in love*.

In love. The idea of being in love sounded about as remote as me running for Prime Minister of Tonga, or sailing the Atlantic single-handed in a teacup, or ever waking up with my hair not sticking out at weird angles.

"Wham-blam love only ever happens in movies," Mum explained, going cross-eyed and spotting the feathery bit on the end of her nose. "But then they've only got an hour and a half to tell a story, so if they make people fall in love wham-blam, it saves a lot of time."

"Well, if it's not wham-blam, what does it feel like?" I asked her, watching as she dusted another potentially feathery bit of kitchen towel across her nose.

"Um … well, I guess you go through the crush stage, and then you spend more and more time hanging out together. Then one day when you're not with the other person, you realize that you miss them; that you would rather hang out with them than anyone else. Then you *know* you're in love."

"Wow…" I nodded.

Well, I definitely hadn't been in love with Keith or Feargal, then. I couldn't wait to get away from either of them, mainly 'cause I hadn't a clue what to talk to them about when we were on our own. I mean, Feargal was all right now; now that he was just a sort of mate. (Course, he might be more of a regular mate for my whole crowd soon, the way that Kyra was chasing after him ever since we'd come back from the geography field trip...)

"But who knows?" Mum yawned, stretching her arms above her head, so all her bright painted wooden bangles slipped down towards her elbows with a clang. "Maybe it's like riding a bicycle."

"Huh?"

"Well, you know what they say: if you fall off a bicycle, you should get back on it straight away before you lose your bottle. Maybe it'd be the best thing for Billy – falling in love again straight away!"

Good grief, I couldn't take in all these different explanations about love at one time. I mean, I could do the advice and the sympathy, but somehow I didn't think I'd manage to arrange for Billy to get a new girlfriend, just like that.

"Think I'll just stick to feeding him HobNobs," I told Mum, making a mental note to hide a few away in a secret place for myself before he came round again.

"*Huuuurrrungghhh!*" snorted Dad in his sleep.

"Ah, look! He's drooling!" Mum smiled, as though it was the cutest thing she'd ever seen.

Help! She must really be in love not to mind anything *that* disgusting...

Chapter 3

CAMERA, ACTION, POODLE

Doggy heaven: that's the park all around Alexandra Palace.

At the sight of all that unlimited greenness, every single dog – no matter how ancient in doggy years it is – turns into a bounding, bouncing, panting puppy.

My lot were no exception. Rolf (lanky, long-legged scruffbucket), Winslet (grumpy, squat-legged scruffbucket) and Ben (handsome, smiley golden retriever) were lolloping off across the wide expanses of grass at high speed. Course they weren't just lolloping for the sheer joy of lolloping; they were also trying very hard to run away from the small, yappy rat in a sheep costume that was on their tail(s). OK, OK, so Billy's dog Precious is a poodle, and I'm probably giving rats a bad name by comparing them to Billy's deeply annoying mutt…

"So, anyway," I carried on with my chattering, as I watched the dogs vanish into a thicket of trees, "Tor's school fête is on from 12 till 4 next Saturday."

"Right…"

The peak of Billy's baseball cap bobbed up and down as we stomped up a grassy incline, vaguely heading in the direction the dogs had gone.

"And me and Rowan said we'd help, 'cause Tor is planning to do this stall of … I dunno … *stuff*."

Bob-bob-bob went the baseball cap.

"Mum's already said she'll be helping out – all the parents are supposed to if they can – but she thinks it'll be too much work for just her and Tor, specially since Ivy'll be there and we'll all have to take turns looking after her."

"Uh-huh."

I knew Billy wasn't listening, but that didn't stop me. Yeah, it would have annoyed me normally, but it was so nice not to have to speak about the Big Split for a while that I wouldn't have minded if Billy began *yawning* at what I was saying, or started *sleepwalking* his way around the park with me this Sunday morning.

"I mean, Grandma and Stanley offered to babysit Ivy, but Tor told her there's going to be a bouncy castle on the day, so there's no *way* she's going to miss out on that."

That baseball cap went right on bobbing.

"And anyway, Grandma and Stanley are going to be too busy decorating the house for Tor's birthday

tea while we're all out. Not that Tor knows that –
it's a surprise."

"Right…"

Up ahead of us, Rolf, Ben and Winslet came
tearing out of the other side of the thicket. There
was no sign of Precious, but we could (sadly) still
hear him yappity-yappity-yapping from somewhere
deep amongst the trees.

"Anyway, the fête thing should be a right laugh,"
I carried on, swinging the dogs' leads in my hand.
"Kyra and Chloe and everyone are all going to
come along. And did I tell you that Jen's dad's
band is going to be playing?"

"Band? What band? Who's playing? Where?"

Ah, so a mention of music jarred him out of the
doldrums. It was good to know that Billy's poor,
befuddled brain was capable of focusing on something else apart from the humiliation of being
chucked by Sandie. Pity he hadn't been listening
properly and was about to be disappointed. Mr
Hudson's band hardly compared to having the Red
Hot Chili Peppers turn up at a primary school
fund-raising fête.

"Don't get too excited!" I warned him. "I'm
talking about Jen's dad's band! They play corny old
folk music or something – remember?"

The hopeful look of interest faded from Billy's

face, and he went back to staring at his trainers scuffing along the grass.

"Oh, *them*. Right."

None of us had seen Jen's dad play, but she'd stuck on a tape of his music once and it was … well, it was the sort of fiddledy, diddly stuff that gave us all the giggles. Even Jen. When her mum shouted through to ask what we were laughing at, Jen had had to switch off the music and try and come up with a fib pretty quick, only she couldn't, 'cause she was laughing so much. I guess Mrs Hudson thought we were all insane. (How true…)

But me and my mates were now desperate to cop a load of Jen's dad's band, just so we could nosey at the ukulele player, who Mr Hudson had fallen in love and moved in with. Maybe Jen was back on speaking terms with her dad and had almost, *maybe*, started to get used to the idea that he wasn't going to get back with her mum, but that wasn't to say she forgave him. And the idea of being with us and slagging off the ukulele player cheered her up no end.

"So are you going to come?"

"Huh?" Billy asked, scrunching up his nose and staring at me, all confused, like I'd just spouted something in ancient Hebrew.

"ARE … YOU … COMING … TO … THE …

FÊTE … THING … NEXT … SATURDAY!" I said loudly and slowly, as if I was speaking to someone who was hard of thinking.

"What fête thing?" Billy blinked at me.

Aaaarrrgghhhh…

Luckily for Billy, something distracted me before I reached over and strangled him with my bare hands. It was a whole kerfuffle of people huddled around a particularly pretty hawthorn tree that my dogs were fond of peeing on. And kerfuffle of people or no kerfuffle of people, it looked like Rolf, Winslet and Ben were determined to keep up their routine.

"Are they a film crew?" asked Billy, perking up now that he'd spotted what I had – the two cameras, the sound guy holding the boom above his head, practically everyone holding clipboards.

"Yeah – haven't you heard that they were around?" I asked, then realized that even if a camera had been three centimetres away from his ear on Crouch End Broadway this week, if he'd been in one of his I've-just-been-chucked blue moods he wouldn't have noticed a thing.

Poor Billy…

"Don't suppose they want our dogs in their programme," I continued, starting to hurry forward, same as Billy, now that a harassed film crew person or two was attempting to shoo the pooches away. What if it was a tender love scene they were shooting? Some guy and some girl leaning in for a smooch under the tree? Rolf lifting his leg might not give the scene the romantic touch they were looking for…

"ROLF! HERE, BOY!" I cried out, hoping that if he came, the other two would follow.

"Uh-oh… PRECIOUS! THIS WAY! COME ON!" Billy yelled, as his prissy poodle came hurtling out of the trees in hot pursuit of my dogs.

At the sound of our shouts, the dogs knew who was boss – *them*. They didn't take the slightest bit of notice. Urgh … how embarrassing! We were going to have to walk *right* up to the film crew and drag our weeing dogs away from the actors, probably getting tons of dirty looks thrown our way.

"*I* know," mumbled Billy, suddenly rummaging in the pocket of his skater shorts and pulling out an empty crisp packet.

"What are you doing with that?" I frowned at him.

"Luring them with food. They'll think it's a packet of doggy treats."

"But it's empty!"

"*They* don't know that!" he grinned, then gave an ear-splitting whistle and held out the bag, rustling it noisily.

I'm very glad to say that all our dogs were very, very thick (not to mention greedy) and fell for Billy's trick straight away, spinning round and galumphing their way back to us at high speed.

"Y'know, from my window, I could see this part of Ally Pally all lit up last night, with all these guys working up here," I told Billy, while speedily fixing leads to collars as my dumb dogs fought to lick at the empty packet of Worcester sauce crisps.

"Cool," Billy shrugged, wrestling with a wriggling Precious who was ducking and diving away from the lead Billy was trying to put on him.

"Wonder what programme it's for this time?" I wondered idly, as I tried to untangle the tangle of leads my idiot pooches were tying themselves up in.

"Maybe it's a crime thing," suggested Billy, grabbing Precious in a headlock now and finally snapping his lead on.

"Maybe." I shrugged, trying to peer through the circle of film crew and spot the actors. (I couldn't.)

"Yeah," Billy suddenly snarled through gritted teeth, pointing two fingers at Precious's head. "Give us the diamonds like you promised or the dog gets it!"

I guessed Billy was trying to sound like a tough gangster, but his growly croakiness just reminded me of someone in an ad for sore throat lozenges. Still, it was really, truly, *deeply* brilliant to see a glimpse of the old, dopey, daft as a fish Billy. More please!

"Nah, it's not a crime programme. Bet it's a romance!" I suggested, thinking of Rolf weeing on that tree again.

"A romance! How wonderful!" Billy sighed in a stupid, floaty voice, scooping a puzzled Precious up in the air and staring straight at him. "Darling! I love everything about you! Your eyes! Your wet nose! Your meaty-chunks breath! And the way you like to sniff other dogs' bums – it's *adorable*!"

This was brilliant times ten. Not Billy's terrible acting, but just the sheer joy of having the real(ly stupid) Billy back. No moping, no misery, no endless mumblings about Sandie. Yessss! Wow, I'd missed him!

"Then again, maybe it's some historical drama!" I said next, egging him on for more twittery.

"Ah, Lady Lavatoria! How divine to see you!" Billy burbled in a fake, posho voice, bowing low to me (and squashing Precious in his arms at the same time). "You know, your bustle is looking bigger than last time I saw it—"

"*Billy!*" I giggled, turning this way and that as he pretended to check out my bum.

"But tell me, Lady Lavatoria, do you like my stylish new bonnet? Verily, they're all the rage with the ladies in Par*eee*!"

That was it. I was *off*. It wasn't *just* the fact that Billy had plonked Precious on his head that gave me the giggles. It was also the way Billy started sashaying along the path like he was on some nineteenth-century catwalk, wiggling his baggy-shorted hips from side to side while Precious – masquerading as a (live) fur hat – scrabbled his pinky-white paws on Billy's baseball cap, desperate to get a foothold.

And then I saw him stop dead, letting all the silliness and smiles slip away as instantly as water down a plughole. I whipped around quick to see what had shocked the fun out of him.

"Er … hi."

Oh.

In fact, *uh*-oh.

Poor Billy. Seeing your ex-girlfriend for the first time after a bad break-up can never be easy. But it's especially difficult when you're caught monkeying around like a dork, wearing a poodle on your head…

Chapter 4

PINGS AND SPLATS

What is it with little kids?

It's like they've got extra batteries or something. Dogs are the same. Little kids and dogs: they can run and shriek, and bark and play endlessly, and then it's like someone whips out their batteries and they fall totally and completely asleep in panting piles.

At 13, I was obviously getting *well* past it. I'd been playing Dodge the Hose in our back garden for nearly an hour now and I was pooped (not to mention very, very wet). Luckily, Ivy – the current holder of the hose – and Tor were having *way* too much fun charging around and chasing each other and the dogs with jets of water that they didn't even spot me slinking off to sit on the swing and get my breath back.

Resting the side of my head against one of the cool, metal chains (barely) holding our swing in place, I let my mind wander and my clothes drip. I was thinking back to a couple of hours ago, when

Billy met Sandie, and wanted to die. Or at least fall into a very deep hole and disappear…

"What was she even doing in the park?" he'd squawked, once Sandie, her dad and baby sister Bobbie had trundled away, and once his shocked vocal chords had loosened up enough for him to speak/squawk. "She knows me and you always come here on a Sunday morning!"

"Well, it's a free country, I guess," I'd shrugged, not really knowing what else to say for a second.

"Whose side are you on?" Billy had suddenly asked, all hurt.

The answer was, I wasn't on *anybody's* side. But Billy didn't exactly see it that way. After saying the most awkward, clipped "hi"s to each other, Sandie and Billy went utterly, miserably quiet, and only Mr Walker saved the day by bursting the bubble of silence and saying, "So … we'll be seeing you later on, then, for tea, Ally?"

I'd nodded, and a millisecond later it seemed, Sandie, her dad and the buggy headed off. Then I'd felt Billy's eyes glare accusingly at me, as if I'd betrayed him by promising to go hang out at Sandie's for an hour or so and be forced to eat her mum's blahhhh cooking.

"Look, I *was* going to tell you that Sandie invited me round," I'd told him, as he stared hard at me, with hurt in his eyes. "She *is* still my mate, y'know, even if you two *have* broken up!"

And then he sort of crumpled a bit, and I felt terrible, like I'd kicked him in the back of the knees or something.

"How was it ... seeing her, I mean?" I'd asked, more gently.

"Like…"

Billy scrunched up his whole face, as his brain struggled to find the right words.

"It was like my heart sort of went … *ping!*"

"Ping?" I'd frowned at him.

Ping didn't seem right. To me, a ping in the heart department felt pretty nice. My heart always went ping! whenever Alfie sauntered into our house (and straight past me, towards either Rowan or Linn). But then English wasn't Billy's best subject at school (playing football at break-time was). Maybe he needed help coming up with the right phrase.

"Are you sure it wasn't more of a heart-*splat*?" I'd suggested.

"Yes! That's it! That how it felt – like a *splat!*" he'd spluttered excitedly, like I'd cracked some secret-agent code. And then I watched his face suddenly fall, and the sad puppy/wet sock expression slide back into place.

"What's up?" I'd asked him.

Spookily, that was the exact part of this morning's conversation that was running through my head when Linn skirted the water fight and wandered over to ask me, "What's up?"

"Just thinking about Billy," I told her, watching her lean against our paint-peeling garden shed. (Amazing – she didn't even check it for dust or cobwebs. *And* she was smiling. This was so not like her – was she ill?)

"Oh, yeah! Where *is* your shadow today?" she asked, glancing around the garden. "I knew *something* was missing!"

"He's had to go home. His big sister is visiting," I explained, letting my eyes scan Linn's black jeans and fitted white T-shirt, all the time aware that next to her natural (or should that be *un*natural?) neatness I looked as soggy, muddy and scuzzy as one of the dogs did right now.

"The one who lives in France?" Linn asked.

"Yeah, her – Beth."

Other people might be glad to see their big sister after months and months, but Beth's visit wasn't exactly going to help lift Billy's spirits. She always treated Billy as if he was about as interesting as the washing machine and talked to him about as much.

"At least it lets you off the hook for a while. You

must be bored stupid talking about the whole thing with him and Sandie by now!"

"A bit…" I shrugged, lazily pushing myself back and forth on the swing with the toes of my grass-stained trainers. "I was speaking to Mum about it last night. She said maybe it would be better if Billy got another girlfriend, really quickly. But she was only joking."

"Hmm … well, finding a boyfriend or girlfriend doesn't happen just like that, does it?" said Linn, stepping back a little as Winslet stopped close by us and shook herself dry, like a hairy spin-dryer on legs. "Unless you set him up, of course."

"Huh?"

What was she on about? Did she expect me to put a postcard in a newsagent's window? *"Lanky skate-boarding freak (13) seeks new girlfriend to replace old one – call this number now!"*

"You've got loads of friends apart from Sandie. Couldn't you set him up with one of them?"

"But how?" I laughed. "What am I meant to say? 'Hey, Chloe – fancy being Billy's new girlfriend? It would really help him out!'"

"No … not like that!" Linn smiled. "You've got to do it really, really cleverly. Like Mary – she thought Nadia and her cousin Ross would be perfect together…"

Mary and Nadia – they were Linn's best mates, apart from (sigh!) Sir Alfie of Gorgeousness.

"...so anyway, Mary kept telling Nadia how funny and cute Ross was, and then every time Mary saw Ross, she kept mentioning her gorgeous friend Nadia. Mary was so subtle about it, neither of them even sussed out that she was match-making. Then she arranged for Ross to come out one night with all of us, and whoosh! – him and Nadia hit it off, without realizing they'd been set up."

That was *it*? A few crummy compliments drip-fed into a few conversations, and you could get two people *falling* for each other? Before I was able to quiz Linn more about this cunning, undercover match-making malarkey, she got kind of distracted.

"Hey, *nooo*! Don't you *dare*, Tor Love!" giggled Linn all of a sudden, crossing her arms in front of her head in a useless attempt to protect her lovingly straightened hair from the blast of the hosepipe.

You know, I'd have bet 20p and a Mars bar that Linn would have shot straight into the house after that, in a total strop at getting messed up. But no – instead, she kicked off her black suede mules and went chasing Tor and Ivy around the garden in her bare feet. Like crispy noodles being chucked into a vat of oil, the smooth, blondey tendrils around Linn's face were already twisting and spiralling into curls, thanks to the soaking our little bruv had given her, and – *shock!* – she didn't seem to mind.

There was that, *and* the fact that she'd come over specially to see me and voluntarily had a nice conversation with me. I mean, conversations with Linn usually go something like, "Linn, do you like my T-shirt?", with her answering, "Yes, it's very nice. Now go away, I'm busy."

That weird feeling I had yesterday … it must have had *something* to do with the way Linn was acting, because she seemed *eerily* happy at the moment and for Linn that just wasn't normal. Had the fairies come in the night and swapped our very own Grouch Queen for someone laid-back and lovely?

Hey, maybe I'd sneak down to the bottom of the garden at midnight and leave the fairies a little Thank You note…

Chapter 5

A NOT-SO-LOVELY SURPRISE...

In the park earlier, before Billy had gone home to grit his teeth and greet his sister, the final thing he'd said to me in a wibbly voice was, "You and Sandie are going to talk about me tonight, aren't you?"

Well, he was *kind* of right. For a few minutes anyway.

As soon as I got round to her place, Sandie started blushing as pink as she'd been in the park, babbling on about how mortified she was to bump into us earlier, and how she always thought me and Billy walked the dogs more on the *other* side of the park, nearer the old racecourse (normally we did, but today we'd got sidetracked by our dogs trying to pee on the film crew). Anyway, she felt terrible, she said. Did Billy feel terrible? Yep, I'd told her. Then she'd bitten her lip and looked terrible for a second or two, till a smile suddenly snapped on her face and she said, "Want to see some photos?"

"...and *that's* his wardrobe ... and that one's of the *inside* of his wardrobe. Aren't his clothes nice?

Do you think that's a Puma top? It looks like it *might* be a Puma top but you can't see it properly. What do you think, Ally?"

"Er, don't know," I answered, squinting at the photo Sandie was holding under my nose. "Guess it might be. Or not."

"*I* know, I'll ask him when I see him on Wednesday! Anyway, *here's* his desk – the lamp on it is really cool, isn't it?"

I admit I *had* been kind of curious to see the photos Jacob had sent Sandie, just so I could check out where he lived and what his room was like. But after 27 snaps that were practically *identical*, I'd lost the will to live. I'd thought I could *just* about make it through the last eight photos before I fainted with boredom on Sandie's bed, but two seconds ago I spotted *another* small, plastic envelope of photos by her side. Good grief, what next? A whole spool of film on his sock drawer?

There was only one thing to do – let my brain slip into neutral and think about something else while nodding and smiling vacantly at the stuff Sandie was showing me. That, and pray that Mrs Walker would end my agony and shout us through for tea soon. It had to be nearly ready ... the smell of warm, tasteless sludge was drifting through from the kitchen.

But first I had to choose a subject to let my

brain float away on…

"That's Jacob's computer. Nice, isn't it? I like the flat screen. Billy always said he wanted a flat screen. And that's Jacob's pile of games. He's got loads, hasn't he?"

Billy … *that's* what I would think about. Billy and his *next* girlfriend. After all, there was no harm *thinking* about it, was there? And, like Linn had said this afternoon in the garden, her mate Mary had managed to hook her cousin and Nadia up without either of them realizing it. So … not that I was *actually* going to do it, but which of my other mates would I fix Billy up with if I could? Chloe? Definitely not; she was *way* too sarcastic and would totally demolish Billy. Kyra? Ha! I knew Billy would have to be bound, gagged and sedated before he went on a date with her (it would be like a bunny nuzzling up to a boa constrictor). Anyway, Kyra had her sights set on Feargal O'Leary (poor guy). So that left Kellie, Salma and Jen. But then ever since the field trip, Kellie had a bit of a crush on Marc in our class, so that ruled *her* out.

Salma? Jen?

"…and the exhibition sounds great, but *so* sad!"

Yikes – Sandie was suddenly talking about something *else* now. I'd better concentrate and work out what it was.

"Mmmm," I mumbled, hoping that was the sort of response she was expecting. It was. (Phew...)

"Jacob's dying to see this 3D movie that's on at the Science Museum at the same time. He says it's meant to make you feel like you're swimming through the wreckage – that'll be so spooky!"

Aha ... *I* got it. She was talking about the *Titanic* exhibition, where they were showing lots of plates and hairbrushes and other genuine personal stuff they found on the ship after it sunk. And the 3D film she was on about was *Ghosts of the Abyss*, at the IMAX cinema, right next door to the exhibition.

"But you'll just cry," I teased Sandie. "You couldn't stop crying after you watched *Titanic* the movie! Actually you cry every time you see it!"

"Well, all those people died!" she shrugged apologetically. "*And* Leonardo DiCaprio!"

"Erm, girls," Mr Walker suddenly interrupted, sticking his head around the bedroom door. "Tea's ready!"

"OK, Dad!" Sandie nodded, pushing herself up off the bed. "Anyway, Ally, can you come?"

For a second I was confused. What did she mean, could I come? I was already *here*, wasn't I? And her parents would think I was pretty rude if I stayed in her room while they ate their tea...

"On Wednesday, I mean! Can you come to the IMAX and the exhibition and stuff? I'd love it if you came too!"

"But you're going on a date, Sand! You don't want me there!"

"Yes I do!" she begged me, hanging on to my arms and batting her big, blue eyes at me imploringly. "Please, please, *please*, Ally! I'll be too shy with Jacob on my own and you're *sooo* good at telling funny jokes!"

Great. I'd be a cross between a gooseberry and a court jester. How attractive.

"Look, you could take one of the others along too!" Sandie offered, trying anything to persuade me. "Just one though – if it was *all* the girls it would be too weird for Jacob, like he was being ganged up on or something. So just one. As long as it's not Kyra, 'cause—"

"Yeah, I know," I nodded quickly, totally understanding that taking Kyra along to the exhibition was madness. She had the attention span of a bluebottle and would get bored before we'd even found the right hall for the exhibition. And when Kyra gets bored, she tends to entertain herself by being loud and obnoxious (er, *not* great for a date, I guess).

"Girls! The lumpy, tasteless sludge is getting

cold!"* Mrs Walker called through, before I got the chance to tell Sandie if I was up for Wednesday or not.

(*What she actually said was, "Girls! The shepherd's pie is getting cold!", but I definitely think "lumpy, tasteless sludge" is a better description.)

"Do you want some more, Ally?" Mrs Walker asked, picking up a big bowl of pink goo and offering it to me.

"No ... no thanks. I'm full!" I smiled.

Full of brown goo followed by pink goo. It was almost like eating one of Rowan's foodie disasters, but Mrs Walker's teas at least had the advantage of tasting of nothing. Rowan's teas always had *lots* of flavours; usually stuff that didn't actually *go* together.

"Well, this is nice, isn't it!" Mr Walker boomed, as he wiped Bobbie's baby-food goo off her face, hands, clothes and high chair.

That was a funny thing to say: "Well, this is nice, isn't it?" Not funny ha, ha, but funny peculiar. It just wasn't the sort of thing Sandie's dad *said*. It sounded kind of fake.

"Yes, it is nice. Isn't it nice, girls?"

Now that was *Mrs* Walker sounding fake.

Sandie knew it was all a bit odd too; I could tell

by the way she was frowning at both her parents.

"What?" she asked, starting to look worried.

Mr and Mrs Walker carried right on with their fake smiling … and then looked at each other, at which point the fake smiles went a bit wobbly. I spotted Mr Walker give his wife the tiniest of nods, as if he was saying, "Go on! *You* do it!" Mrs Walker opened her eyes a minute bit wider for a split second, like she was answering, "No, why don't *you* do it!" But somehow Sandie's dad won out, and it was her mum who turned the full beam of her fake smile at Sandie and me.

"Well, Sandra, we – me and your dad – have a wonderful surprise!"

Uh-oh … they weren't having another baby, were they? They acted weird and drove Sandie crazy before they finally broke the news that they were expecting Bobbie.

"A surprise?" Sandie blinked warily at her mum. "Like what?"

"Like … we're moving!" Mr Walker blurted out cheerfully. "To Bath!"

I think both me and Sandie felt like we'd just had all the air sucked out of our lungs by aliens. It took a second till either of us got enough breath to speak.

"What, me too?" Sandie asked dumbly (which

was completely understandable, under the circumstances).

"Of *course*, darling!" Mrs Walker laughed. "You, Roberta, me and Dad! All of us are moving to Bath! We're going to live in a beautiful big Georgian house that's twice the size of this place!"

"Er … when?" asked a tiny voice, which happened to be mine.

"Um … that's the *other* part of the surprise," announced Mr Walker, smiling but looking nervous at the same time. "We're moving next Saturday!"

"Isn't that … uh … lovely?" asked Mrs Walker warily.

People react to shock in different ways: some people go quiet, some people get shouty, some people get shivery and some people feel sick. Sandie did all four. First she said nothing, then she shouted, "I hate you!", and then finally she started shivering, *right* before she barfed.

I don't know *how* exactly Sandie's parents expected her to respond to their sledgehammer news, but I kind of think they deserved to spend the evening with Mr Muscle, scrubbing brown and pink goo out of their beige carpet…

Chapter 6

FROM ONE NOT-SO-LOVELY SURPRISE TO ANOTHER

Isn't it maddening when you've got stuff you need to rant about, and no one to rant to?

That's how I felt when I got home from Sandie's, when I walked in and spotted Mum on the phone to her pal Val in Cornwall and Dad in the middle of a bedtime story with Tor. I reckoned Rowan was my next best option, but just before I knocked on her bedroom door, I heard her talking, and realized Alfie must be with her, or maybe it was Von or Chazza (though she hadn't exactly been seeing so much of her inseparable best mates since she and Alfie had become even more inseparable).

So I'd either have to keep my rant to myself for a little while longer, or...

"Hello?" I said warily, surprised to get to the top of the attic stairs and find Linn's door open, instead of barricaded tightly shut (to keep pet hairs, noise, and messy members of the Love family out of her sanctuary).

I also wasn't used to hearing Linn do something

as carefree as sing along to her CDs. And had I actually caught her *dancing*? There was something seriously wrong with that girl. She was having way too much fun.

"Hi, Ally – what's up?" Linn stopped and smiled at me.

(The normal reaction I'd have expected was a terse, "Well? What do you want?")

But much as her new, improved personality was freaking me out, I decided to take advantage of it. I mean, who knew? Maybe she'd wake up next day and be back to her usual Grouch Queen self, snapping at me and Rowan for breathing untidily in her vicinity or something.

"I've just been to Sandie's," I began. "You'll never guess what…"

"What?" asked Linn, smoothing an invisible hair back into her scraped-straight, stubby ponytail.

"Her parents announced that they're moving."

"Moving? Somewhere else around here, or moving away?"

"Away. To Bath. On Saturday."

"Omigod, Ally!" said Linn, looking genuinely shocked and sorry for me and for Sandie. "Come on in – sit down!"

I stepped into her all-white, all-neat room, and looked around for somewhere to perch myself where I wouldn't crease something. (That meant the bed was out.)

"They're moving on *Saturday*? I can't believe that!" Linn gasped, turning down the volume on her CD player. "How can you keep such huge and important news from your own daughter? Are Sandie's parents *mad*?"

"Probably," I muttered settling down on the padded window seat. "They said they thought knowing about it would 'disrupt her concentration at school' or something lame like that. And then they said that they hadn't wanted to tell her too soon, in case it upset her."

"Yeah – like Sandie's *dead* happy about it now, right?" snorted Linn, her voice dripping with sarcasm, as she sat and leant back on her crisp, white duvet cover, propping herself up on her elbows.

"She's thrilled – *not*. She ended up shouting at her mum and dad. She told them she hated them."

From my viewpoint, I saw Colin hover gingerly at Linn's door, as stunned as I was to see it open; open to this practically unknown, pristine room.

"Can't blame her," said Linn, rolling her eyes. "But how could Sandie not have known? Weren't there people coming around to view her place when her parents put it up for sale?"

Over by the doorway, Colin warily sniffed at the

carpet, then padded a tentative paw on it, as if he thought all that smooth creamy-whiteness was ice. Once he realized it was safe and would take his weight, he slowly began to slink his way in (which was pretty good going – slinking's not that easy when you're a cat that's got one less leg than it should have).

"I guess so, but her parents must have arranged for buyers to come when she was at school," I explained, remembering the rushed unhappy conversation I'd just had locked away in Sandie's room. "She told me she only once thought it was weird when this person came to the house, and started noseying around. But her dad told her afterwards that it was just a window cleaner, come to give them a quote. Which Sandie *did* think was weird, considering it was a woman with a little baby..."

"Her parents *are* mad."

"*Tell* me about it. And you know what her dad said to me when he dropped me home just now?"

With a delicate *whumpff!*, Colin bounced up on to Linn's fat, soft, white cloud of a duvet, and began to pad and purr ecstatically.

"What?" asked Linn, absently reaching over to tickle Colin under his drooling chin, instead of shooing him and his cat hairs off her bed like I'd have expected her to.

"He said thanks to me for coming round. He told me him and Sandie's mum had invited me around for tea specially, 'cause they thought me being there would help soften the blow for Sandie."

"So, they're cowards as well as mad?" Linn suggested. "And they might have been thinking – in their own weird way – about Sandie's feelings by asking you round, but I don't suppose they care how *you* might be feeling, having your best mate whisked away at five minutes' notice!"

Urgh...

Me and Sandie, Sandie and me. OK, so I'd got a bit bugged by her recently, with the whole Billy and Jacob thing, but really, that was about as annoying as having an itch on your back that you couldn't quite scratch, i.e. it wasn't a big deal. But me and Sandie, Sandie and me ... us not hanging out any more at my house, us not trudging home together gossiping about the day, us not doing our homework together and dropping biscuit crumbs on our books ... it was too weird. *Way* too weird to get my head around.

"So – dumb question I know – but how *are* you feeling about it, Ally?"

"Like my head's gone twisty," I mumbled, turning and staring out of Linn's window at the view of central London's high-rises off in the distance. I wasn't sure if I felt like crying or not, but I felt pretty sure if Linn looked at me too sympathetically I might just start blubbing anyway.

"A twisty head..." I heard Linn laugh softly. "That's a good way of putting it! I think I've got a bit of a twisty head too!"

"Huh?" I grunted, turning back and staring at her. Linn didn't look or sound like she had much of a twisty head at the moment, not the way she'd been acting the last few days.

"Well, OK – maybe it's not quite twisty," smiled Linn, patting a finger against her temple. "Maybe it's more ... more like someone just let a firework off in there!"

"What are you on about?" I asked bluntly. First she was coming over spookily nice, and now she was whiffling rubbish. That's *my* job – I whiffle the rubbish in this family. Linn is the smart one who talks in plain, sensible (slightly grumpy) sentences.

"Well, you know how I couldn't make up my mind what to do at university?"

She might not have decided what exactly to study, but what my big sister was going to do at university was be *brilliant*. In all her exams and tests at school so far, she'd scored high, high, high, and all for scary subjects like science and maths and psychology and stuff.

"Have you decided now?" I asked her, feeling curious. It was bound to be quantum physics or criminal psychology or something impressive.

"Yes!" Linn nodded, suddenly pushing herself up on the bed and making Colin nearly jump out of his hairy cat suit. "I've been thinking it over and over for ages, but just this last week, I've been talking it over loads with my careers adviser, and now I'm really sure!"

"Sure about what exactly?"

"Ally..." Linn grinned at me, her eyes shining with excitement, "...next year I'm going to apply to the dental school in Edinburgh!"

"What for?" I asked, temporarily bamboozled.

"To do dentistry, dum-dum!" Linn laughed.

DENTISTRY! My brain suddenly shrieked. *EDINBURGH!*

It was all too much; was *everyone* I loved planning to move away from Crouch End...?

Chapter 7

BEAUTIFUL BUT MENTAL

The new shrine in the corner of Rowan's room was mental. Beautiful, but mental.

She'd copied the idea for it from a magazine article about Mexico – apparently it's very popular there to have a shrine (to Jesus and Mary and any random saints you happen to be fond of) in the corner of your room. It sounds pretty sombre and depressing, but it's not at all – they decorate it with as much colourful, gaudy tat as they can lay their hands on. If you think Rowan's room's bizarre, with its raspberry walls, junk shop bits, fairy lights and home-made works of "art", you'd be blown away by some of those shrines. It's like, there'll be some big picture of Jesus with a few fat cherubs swanning around his head, surrounded by *more* pictures and statuettes, as well as *heaps* of candles, *tons* of flowers (real and fake), *gallons* of fruit (real and fake) and reams and *reams* of tinsel or fairy lights. When you see one of these shrines (and Rowan showed me the magazine article when

I walked in her room and gasped) it makes you kind of wonder why someone like my sister had never made herself one before now.

"Hey, maybe she's decided on dentistry 'cause of the uniform!" Rowan suddenly suggested, as she picked bits of melted, purple wax and sequins off her fingers.

We'd been discussing Linn's shock announcement, as you might expect. And what Ro had just said was true; dentists had to wear those spotless, fitted white coats, didn't they?

"Actually, it's dead perfect for her!" Rowan continued, warming to her theme, now that she'd got over being gobsmacked at Linn's news. "You have to wear your hair scraped back all neat. And you have to put on a face mask, for germs and stuff, and Linn *hates* germs. And the whole job is fiddly and precise, with all those tiny, delicate, sterilized tool thingies. It's just all so totally *her*!"

Rowan might have fluff, feathers and sequins for brains, but she was right. I'd been so stunned when Linn told me about her plans that it hadn't dawned on me that for Linn – a born perfectionist (raised in a house full of scruffs) – the idea of tidying up untidy mouths would be pure heaven.

Only why did she have to go and train to do it in *Edinburgh*? I knew the Grouch Queen always got wound up about living in our chaotic, messy house, but was she *that* desperate to get far, far away from us? (Answer: yes – very, very probably.)

Now that Tor was in snoozeland and Mum was off the phone, Linn had gone downstairs to break the news to our parents. After she'd padded off to do the deed, I'd felt so antsy (in my pantsy) that I decided to try giving Rowan a knock, in the hope that her visitors had vamoosed and we could talk.

It turned out that Rowan hadn't had visitors in the first place – when I'd heard her voice earlier, she was busy yakking to Johnny Depp, of all people. *Yep*, Johnny Depp. Not quite in the flesh, sadly for Rowan (he was her hero – the weirder the film role he played the more she adored him). Instead, Ro had been chattering away to one of the many pictures of him that she'd gathered over the years, welcoming him to his new shrine corner.

Oh, yes. Instead of some saint, she'd made a shrine for Johnny. But that was the only change she'd made. Apart from Johnny Depp being the main focus of attention, she had just as much colourful, gaudy tat as any Mexican shrine. There were the candles (spluttering nicely now, and hand-dotted with sequins), the flowers (all fake, all eye-meltingly bright colours), the fruit (all plastic, left over from when she decorated our house in a tropical stylee in the summer), and the fairy lights, rearranged and reassembled from different parts of her room. Oh, and I forgot to mention the weird, mad little dolls and trolls she'd placed on the shrine instead of religious statuettes. She'd bought the whole lot of 'em for 27p from a garden-gate sale some nine-year-old kids were holding down our street a couple of weeks ago. (Ro hadn't come up with the shrine idea at that point, but bought the dolls and trolls anyway just 'cause she'd thought they'd "come in handy". Strange girl...)

"We only just got Mum back – I don't want Linn to go!" I moaned, staring at the candlelight dancing across Ro's favourite picture of Johnny done up as Edward Scissorhands (*not* a good look, trust me).

"Yeah, but she hasn't applied yet, and she might not get in. And even if she gets in, she wouldn't be going there for a whole other year!" Rowan assured me, acting for once in her life like my older sister (by two years). Still, it was hard to take her seriously when her hair was full of mad, bendy, pink and purple sponge ... *things*, that would presumably give her ringlets in the morning (and make her look like a fruitcake tonight).

Actually, speaking of fruitcake, her purple bendy roller things matched the purple candle wax and sequins attached to her fingers. Maybe

Rowan was a disorganized disaster zone next to the perfection of Linn, but at least she *matched*, in her own weird way...

"OK, fair enough," I muttered, trying to take on board what Ro was saying. But it was hard, coming on top of Sandie's news. If anyone else told me today that they planned to move away – if Britney our adopted pigeon even so much as cooed about flapping off on migration – I'd take it very, very badly.

"Hey!" Rowan suddenly said enthusiastically, as she wiped her waxy, sequinned fingers on her over-sized dungarees. "Why don't we sneak downstairs and see how Linn's getting on?"

I hadn't known how exactly Rowan would take the news of Linn heading up to Scottish-land (where her name – her full name of Linnhe – came from). Linn, being so ferociously sensible, often gave Rowan, being so ferociously airheady, a really hard time. But Rowan had been great. She'd been pretty stunned at Linn's news (she'd even dropped the troll she'd been sticking sequins on to when I told her), then she'd started wittering on about how dentistry and Linn went together like Pot Noodle and a copy of *Heat*.

And so, thirty seconds later, me and Rowan found ourselves propped outside the living-room door, earwigging while trying to shush two cats that weren't Colin from doing some major volume manic purring, and practically holding our hands over Rolf's snout to stop him from happily barking at the sight of us. (Why can't he act more like Ben and just grin when he sees us? Or maybe that's just something golden retrievers can do…)

"Look, I love Edinburgh, and so does Melanie – I mean, your mum… We can totally see why you'd want to go there!" we heard Dad say.

"Absolutely! Edinburgh is beautiful and amazingly historic," we heard Mum say next, "and its universities are brilliant. It would be great to be a student there."

"But?"

That was Linn, obviously reading between the lines of what Mum and Dad were saying.

For a brief few seconds, no one spoke. And then Dad came out with something that Linn *really* didn't want to hear…

"The thing is, Linn, love … I just don't think we can afford for you to go to university in Edinburgh. You know how tight things are for us when it comes to money."

Oh no. OK, so maybe I didn't want Linn to go away, but then I didn't want her *not* to be able to go, if you see what I mean.

"But, Dad, the dental school has a brilliant reputation! And I know you don't have loads of money to send me there, but I've been saving from my Saturday job and I could get a weekend job or something when I'm studying in Edinburgh!"

"It's not just the fees, though, is it, Linnhe?" Mum butted in gently. "It's the actual cost of just *living*. If you go to university in London, then we'll manage fine; we can save for the fees over the next year, and you'll be living at home so there won't be any extra expense there."

Urgh. Mum and Dad didn't get it, did they? It wasn't just the brilliant course that was drawing Linn to Edinburgh, it was the chance to be independent, out on her own, away from all of us, as much as she (hopefully) loved us. Linn could just about cope with one more year living at home while she was finishing sixth form and A levels, but being stuck here for another four years after that? It would probably drive her – and us – certifiably insane.

"Your dad's right – Edinburgh's nearly as expensive to live in as London. You'd need to take out such a huge student loan, you'd be paying it back for years!"

Linn wasn't saying anything.

"Ooof…" mumbled Rowan quietly, tuning into Linn's crushing, silent disappointment just like me.

"Linn, sweetheart, if we had the money…"

"Like your dad says, if we had the money, we'd love for you to go, but—"

"Look, it's OK, Mum," Linn interrupted her bluntly, although I think the bluntness was probably down to Linn trying to keep herself from crying. "I understand. It's fine."

As her feet stomped speedily towards the door, Ro and me looked at each other in a panic and bounded up the stairs two at a time, hurtling ourselves into Ro's room before we were caught earwigging.

"Poor Linn…" Rowan whispered, as we listened to our big sister thunder up the staircase.

"Rolf! Ben! Out of my way!" we heard her hiss angrily as she passed Ro's door.

Uh-oh. I did feel truly, horribly sorry for Linn, but this didn't mean the Grouch Queen was back, did it? I'd liked the new, improved, non-grumpy Linn and was really going to miss her…

Chapter 8

SHOOING BILLY

Quite a few people in Priory Park were standing stock-still, with their mouths hanging open. Well, it's a sedate swings 'n' ice-creams 'n' rose-beds type park and and you don't expect to see a crashed car with smoke billowing out of it stuck in one of those rose-beds. Or a camera crew ringed around it, filming every angle.

Billy and Kyra certainly had their mouths hanging open, but it had nothing to do with the future telly programme being put together – which was quite something when you think how starstruck Kyra was with the whole lights, camera, action thing going on. (She'd come to meet me in the park dressed in her best jeans and cropped T-shirt, just to help boost her chances of being talent-spotted, I supposed.)

"You are *kidding*!" gasped Kyra, staring hard at me for signs of kidding.

Billy wasn't saying anything. He wasn't even moving. I think he was so shocked at what I'd just told him and Kyra that I could have parked the end of my empty Coke bottle in his gob and he wouldn't have flinched.

"Nope. Sandie's definitely moving – this Saturday. Cross my heart and hope to die."

"But … but this is Monday *already*! Wow – she must be *gutted*!" exclaimed Kyra, wrinkling her nose up, so her dark freckles almost disappeared in the light brown folds of her skin.

"Totally," I nodded.

"Poor Sandie…"

As she mumbled, Kyra looked pretty gutted herself. I guess it was 'cause she'd had to move plenty of times, and knew how hard it was to leave everything and start again, somewhere strange and not necessarily welcoming.

Billy still wasn't responding. It was as if someone had pressed a pause button on him (under his baseball cap, maybe?). Meanwhile, not far from us, it looked like the special effects had got a bit *too* special. The car was billowing out unexpectedly *huge* amounts of black smoke (you could tell it was unexpected from the way all the production team were running around looking hassled and worried). Instead of hovering around noseying at the telly people, young mums were now coughing and pushing buggies away at top speed, and spluttering old people were hurrying off as fast as they could (which wasn't very fast), as the black smoke smothered everything around it. Normally, Billy would have thought the sight of something going wrong like this was excellent fun ("Cool!"), but today, the old bowling green in the park could have lifted up to reveal an underground bunker for Thunderbirds 4 and he wouldn't have (couldn't have) batted an eyelid.

"Is she upset?" Kyra asked me, looking upset.

"*Really* upset."

I wouldn't have been surprised if Sandie had cried herself to sleep about moving away. I knew for a fact that my sister Linn was crying last night – about *not* moving away. It was just after I'd left Mum and Dad and gone back to my room that I heard her. I stopped outside her bedroom door and wondered if I should knock, but I thought Linn would probably want to be left alone. I didn't suppose she'd be too thrilled to have someone (i.e. me) stare at her when her eyes and nose were swollen, puffy and red and her mascara had drizzled down her cheeks. (Linn might hate mess, but even *she* can't arrange to cry neatly.) Feeling useless, I'd just tiptoed to my room, avoiding standing on the squeaky floorboard, or the snoring Winslet, so that I didn't disturb or embarrass my eldest sis.

"I'll phone Sandie when I get back…"

"Yeah, it would be good if you could," I told Kyra, thinking that unlike Linn, Sandie would be desperate for company and sympathy.

I sneaked a peek at Billy, wondering how he was taking the news. Obviously he was shocked. But what exactly was going on in that brain of his? Was he devastated 'cause it meant there was no chance of them ever getting back together? How horrible and tragic and sad if that was what was trundling through his mind. Or was he thinking he should talk to Sandie before she went, so there'd be no hard feelings? That would be brilliant – for *me*, apart from anyone else. This week was going to be a toughie, if I had to carry on babysitting Billy *and* try and cram in quality hanging-out time with Sandie. It would be so much easier – for *me*, like I say – if they were back on speaking terms…

"You all right?" Kyra suddenly nudged Billy in the ribs.

Urgh. Kyra Davies is about as subtle as a herd of stampeding buffaloes in clogs. While I'd been trying to work out a tactful way of sussing out how Billy was taking Sandie's news, Kyra waded right in there with an in-yer-face question and a pointy elbow.

"Yeah, I'm OK," Billy shrugged unconvincingly, hitching his skateboard up to his chest as if it was a shield (smart idea, considering Kyra's sharp elbows). "I was just thinking about my sister, that's all."

Well, that was a lie, if ever I heard one. But if Billy didn't want to talk about Sandie – in front of Kyra, I guessed – then hey, I understood. I'd even play along. (That's what friends are for – to help you hide your excruciating embarrassment, amongst other things.)

"How's it going with Beth?" I asked him. "Is she ignoring you, as usual?"

"I *wish*!" he grunted. "She just keeps sort of *snorting* at me!"

"Snorting?" Kyra snorted at him. "What are you on about?"

"You know ... *I* say something, then *she* looks at me like I've got a cabbage for a head and Smash for brains. And then she snorts."

"What sort of stuff are you saying to her?" I asked warily. Billy can come out with some top-notch drivel (example: two weeks ago he laughed himself stupid telling me about how him and Hassan filled Stevie's football boots full of mud). Maybe Billy had been spouting such total rubbish to Beth that the poor girl couldn't help herself. Though from what I remembered of her being a snotty, distant moo over the years, I doubted it.

"Well, I've only said three things to Beth since she got home."

"Which were?" I quizzed him.

"Um ... 'Hello' ... 'Can you pass the salt?' and 'Are you going to eat that kebab?'"

Fair enough. All quite reasonable, if slightly greedy. But nothing that particularly deserved a sarcastic snort.

"Where did you say she lived?" asked Kyra.

"Paris. Wish she'd go back there. Soon."

"How long is she home for anyway?"

"Dunno. She got mad when Mum asked her so *I'm* not going to risk it."

Just as Billy stopped speaking, a siren at the nearby fire station started up with a wail. And then we realized that the wailing wasn't coming from the fire station – it was coming from a fire engine that was hurtling through the park gates in the direction of the film set. Over by the car, the smoke kept pouring at an alarming rate, while production staff ran about flapping their clipboards uselessly and a couple of blokes pointed weeny, hopelessly undersized extinguishers in the vague direction of some unscripted fire that had broken out.

"Excellent!" said a voice, as a skateboard rattled to a stop beside us.

"Cool!" said another voice, followed by a screech of not-quite-burning rubber as a second skateboard skidded to a halt.

It was Billy's mates Hassan and Stevie, wearing matching Quiksilver skater shorts and T-shirts, and matching grins of excitement at seeing the small disaster unfold in front of us.

"We're going up the skate park at Ally Pally. Coming?" Hassan asked, without bothering to look at any of us, which might have helped us work out who he was talking to. But then again, him and Stevie hadn't even bothered to say *hello*, so what was new?

"I think he's talking to *you*," I told Billy, as we all stood and gawped at the fire crew doing their thing. (The guy who looked like he might be the director was slowly thumping his head against a nearby tree as a hose began to rain water all over his set. Bang went today's shoot, I guess.)

"Nah," mumbled Billy, replying to either me or Hassan. "I'm all right. I'm just hanging out with Ally."

He was talking to Hassan, then.

"*Course* he wants to go with you," Kyra suddenly butted in. "Go on, Billy! It'll be a laugh!"

"But…" Billy fumbled for words, wondering why Kyra was so keen to shove him off with his mates. (Which was something *I* was kind of wondering myself.)

"Look – the fire's nearly out. There's nothing else to gawp at," Kyra announced, pointing towards the car. "See you guys later!"

I had absolutely no idea what she was up to.

"Yeah, come on, Billy!" said Stevie, flipping his skateboard upright with the toe of his trainer and grabbing it in his hand.

"But I told Ally I'd—"

"Listen, Billy, I really need to talk to Ally alone … about *girl* stuff."

At Kyra's mention of "girl" stuff, all three boys started shuffling and coughing and looking very uncomfortable.

"Uh, OK…" shrugged Billy. "Catch you later, then, Al?"

And with that he sloped off after Stevie and Hassan, throwing a glance at me over his shoulder, a glance that made him look as sad as a stray dog that's just been shooed off in the rain…

"*What* girl stuff?" I turned and asked Kyra, determined to find out what she was up to now that the boys were out of earwigging range.

"Nothing," she said brightly. "I was just trying to get rid of Billy. For his own good."

"How come?"

"Well, he's still all mopey about Sandie, isn't he? And if he mooches around with you – *again* – he's just going to end up talking about it all – *again*. He needs to take his mind off it all by hanging out with his stupid *boy* mates for a while."

"I guess so," I mumbled, relieved to be getting time off from being Billy's unpaid agony aunt. But still, I couldn't help feeling sorry to see him go. I guess… Well, I s'pose I was sort of guilty, like I wasn't doing my job and looking out for him properly. Or something.

"I mean, clattering about on their dumb skate-boards, comparing spots: *that's* the sort of stuff Billy needs to be doing to take his mind off Sandie!"

Kyra was right, I decided, trying not to picture Billy's stray puppy dog face and pleading eyes. He might not have wanted to go with Stevie and Hassan, but it was a case of being cruel to be kind.

Y'know, Kyra acting all considerate; who'd have thought it?

"Gold star to you for being so nice to Billy!" I smiled at her, while trying to offload my guilty conscience.

"*Nice?*" she snorted, her eyes glued to the firemen, as they began to retract their hose. "You've *got* to be joking! I just couldn't *stand* hearing any more about Sandie and them splitting up! If he'd started up about her when I was around, I'd have had to *shoot* myself with the sheer boredom of it all!"

How thoughtful and kind Kyra was – *not*!

"And now I don't have to pretend to be interested in listening to Billy," she babbled on, smoothing her hair back and fixing her light-brown, almond eyes on someone with a clipboard, "I can maybe go and see if I can wangle a bit part in whatever they're filming!"

Ah, now *that* was the selfish, thoughtless, conniving Kyra I knew and (sort of) loved...

Chapter 9

JEALOUSY AND GENEROUSNESS

So much for "Catch you later, Al!"

I didn't hear from Billy for the rest of the day, which meant he'd either a) had a brilliant time with Hassan and Stevie up at the skateboard park at the back of Ally Pally, or b) decided I was a cruel and heartless best mate for sending him away and he was sulking badly with me, all hurt and alone. I hoped it was a), but the niggling worry that it was b) was putting me off my food tonight, which was a waste because it was Mum's home-made Mexican (i.e. hot and spicy enough to melt your tongue).

Mum had gone to the trouble of making the Mexican meal (roly pancakes and all) in honour of Sandie coming for tea. Mexican is Sandie's absolute favourite food, probably because of all the tasteless gloop she has to suffer at home. Grandma and Stanley weren't so keen – after a couple of mouthfuls Grandma had a frosty expression on her face and was ladling on *huge* dollops of cooling sour cream, while Stanley practically had white-hot *steam* coming out of his hairy ears.

"Didn't Alfie want to stay for tea? There's plenty!" Mum asked Rowan, who was currently tossing back her mad bundle of ringlets and slipping into the chair opposite me.

Ro had just been saying bye to the splendiferously gorgeous Alfie, so there'd probably been a massive snogathon happening on our doorstep just now.

"No, he didn't want to," Rowan explained, surprisingly brightly. "He's not really talking to me!"

OK, so no snogathon, then.

"*Why* isn't he talking to you?" asked Dad, through a mouthful of something oozing salsa.

Everyone around the table was staring at Ro, waiting for the answer (everyone except Ivy, who had wriggled under the table to feed individual grains of rice to the dogs). I checked out Linn's reaction in particular: maybe she'd accepted it, but she'd never been exactly zippedy-doo-dah happy about her best mate and her sister dating. And so yeah, Linn *was* looking at Rowan – same as the rest of us – but her expression was pretty blank, oddly enough.

"He's gone off in a huff over my Johnny Depp shrine! Can you believe it?"

"You mean, he's *jealous*," stated Grandma, in her usual, let's-cut-to-the-chase, plain-speaking way.

"Imagine the lad getting jealous over a few pictures!" Stanley laughed. (Imagine an old bloke looking like his head was going to explode over a spicy burrito.)

"I *know*!" squeaked Rowan indignantly. "OK, so I *love* Johnny Depp, and OK, so I made a *shrine* to him. But what's the big deal?"

"Maybe you should offer to make a shrine to Alfie in another corner of your room!" Dad suggested cheerily.

"Can I see it? The shrine, I mean?" asked Sandie, wide-eyed.

"Sure! I just made a new frame for a photo of him from *Pirates of the Caribbean* today – it's a whole bunch of jelly babies glued into a heart shape!"

Wow, Sandie was *really* going to miss my family. Not just Ro and her weird art and even weirder fashion sense, but Tor and Dad and Mum and Ivy and Linn too. Most of the time we were all messy and ridiculous (Grandma and Linn excepted), but at least we were interesting. I knew Sandie was my best mate, but I often felt she was half in love with the Love family in general…

"Maybe it'll give you ideas for things to do in your new bedroom, Sandie!" Mum smiled at her, while dolloping more guacamole on her plate.

"Maybe," Sandie shrugged, looking a bit downcast all of a sudden at the mention of her move.

"Look, I know it's been a bit of a shock, but you shouldn't get too down about moving to Bath," Mum tried to comfort her, spotting the telltale signs of gloom in Sandie's body language. "It isn't exactly on the other side of the world – you and Ally will still be able to see each other!"

"Where's Bath?" asked Tor, glancing up from the mountain range he was moulding out of refried beans.

"An hour or so away by train," Dad chipped in, "so Ally can go and visit really easily!"

"And Bath is a wonderful city, Sandie. It's so full of history, and it's very busy and bustling, being a university town!"

What Grandma had just said – she didn't realize it, but she could have been describing Edinburgh (er … if she'd said "Edinburgh" instead of "Bath", of course). I wasn't the only one who seemed to think that – maybe it was all just a bit too close for comfort as far as Linn was concerned.

"Um, listen," Linn announced, standing up and screeching her chair back. "I think I'm getting a migraine, so I'm just going to go to my room, if that's OK."

"Of course it's OK!" Mum nodded, looking concerned.

As Linn bolted from the table, Rowan glanced my way. She knew, same as me, that Linn didn't have a migraine – just a serious case of total disappointment. That, and a case of claustrophobia at the idea of being forced to live with us messy lot for another zillion years...

"What's the matter?" asked Tor, catching sight of Mum and Dad's troubled faces.

"Is she ill? Is there something wrong?" Grandma frowned, her voice low, even though we'd just heard Linn thunder up the stairs and slam her door shut with a reverberating thud.

"She's just not very happy, that's all," said Mum sadly. "We've had to let her down. Badly."

"Yep," Dad nodded sadly. "Linn wanted to apply to dental school in Edinburgh next year, but we told her that we just can't afford it."

No one spoke for a second, as everyone (who hadn't heard it before) digested the news. Only Rolf slurping frantically from the water bowl broke the silence. (Someone, sometime would have to explain to Ivy that feeding the dogs blobs of chilli was sort of *cruel*.)

"Oh dear, oh dear, oh dear..." Grandma sighed, speaking for us all in those six words.

"*I* know!" Tor piped up, his Malteser eyes shining.

"You know *what*, sweetheart?" asked Mum.

"I don't want any birthday presents!" our little brother blurted out. "So all the money you were going to spend on me next Saturday, you can give it to Linn so she can go away to Edinburgh!"

It was a really nice thought, and I'm not sure how much money everyone had planned to spend on Tor's birthday, but the novelty dog bowl (with ears) that I had my eye on only cost £7.99. And I may be spectacularly rubbish at maths, but even *I* knew that £7.99 wasn't exactly going to help pay for Linn to stay in Edinburgh for four years.

I wished and hoped that someone would magically come up with a better suggestion than Tor's, but from the sad smiles going on around the table, it didn't look like any lucky fairy dust would be twinkling into Linn's life and making all her dreams come true any time soon…

Chapter 10

THE LAST SLEEPOVER

Two best friends … a beautiful view … a lot of memories … and a gently snoring dog. Oh, yes, it was Monday night, we were in my bedroom and it was Sandie's last ever sleepover at mine. (Blub!)

Without agreeing to it out loud, we'd both been doing our best to avoid talking about dodgy subjects (i.e. moving away and Billy). Instead, we'd yakked about daft stuff like my ongoing not-quite-kissing dream ("What if it's not Alfie? What if you find out it's someone yucky, like Mr Horace?" Sandie had teased me cruelly. Me, snogging our bad-breathed, bad-tempered maths teacher? I'd rather snog Spartacus the tortoise…).

"So what did Kyra say they were filming again?" asked Sandie, over the sound of Rolf's noisy zzzzzs.

"Some boring police drama thing," I told her, as we leant our pyjama'd elbows on my bedroom window sill, staring off through the dark, street-lamp-spangled night in the direction of Ally Pally.

The Palace wasn't lit up tonight, but the grounds were; there was an arc of white somewhere over by the Pitch 'n' Putt. (Maybe the criminals in this police drama liked to relax with a little late-night golf after their crime-filled days?)

"Kyra's so brave, the way she just goes straight up to people and asks them stuff, isn't she?"

Unlike Sandie, I wasn't sure if I'd exactly describe Kyra as brave; more just plain nosey and downright cheeky (and desperate to get in view of a camera lens). Still, it was quite handy having a nosey, cheeky, desperate-to-be-famous mate – I guess I'd been kind of curious about the filming, and today in the park, once the crew had started tidying up after the fire engine left, Kyra zoomed right on over and asked one of the frazzled members of staff what was going on. "It's a pro-gramme about roller-blading vampires," she'd told me once she'd sashayed back. "*Is* it?" I'd gasped, suddenly intrigued. "*No!*" Kyra had laughed in my face. "It's just a dull cops 'n' robbers thing."

Did I mention that Kyra is nosey, cheeky *and* a complete wind-up merchant?

"Bor-*iiinnggg*," I'd rolled my eyes at Kyra's news. "You wouldn't want a part in that anyway, would you?"

"Of *course* I would!" Kyra frowned at me in

surprise. "I'd be up for appearing in a *toilet* cleaner advert if someone would have me!"

"So ... did you ask if that lot needed any extras?" I'd quizzed her, while wondering how you could do a walk-on part in a toilet cleaner ad (there don't tend to be many people strolling around in the background in your average bathroom).

"Yes ... and the bloke said they've got all the extras they need. Not that I'm going to let *that* stop me. I mean, I could just cruise around Crouch End and find out where they're filming every day, and hang around till I get spotted, couldn't I?"

Er ... yeah, *right*. Did I mention that Kyra is nosey, cheeky, a complete wind-up merchant and strangely *deluded*?

"Y'know, I wish I was brave like Kyra," Sandie sighed now, propping her chin up on the heels of her hands. "Then I could just come out with it and tell Mum and Dad that I'm not moving to Bath!"

"That'd be pretty difficult, Sand. They'd have to *un*-sell your place and *un*-buy the house in Bath, and I don't think *that's* going to happen!"

"Oh, *they* could still move, Ally! But I'd stay here – with you lot!"

I knew Sandie was just fooling around, but unknown to her, my family used to joke about her trying to secretly move in with us. It wasn't just the amount of times she was round at our place (I think the neighbours thought there were *four* teenage Love sisters), it was also 'cause we'd find her toothbrush in with ours, or her homework down the back of the sofa, or her socks in the washing basket.

"Yeah, we could empty all the grot out of the attic cupboard next door, and that could be *your* room!" I carried on the joke.

The attic cupboard was about the size of a peanut, and rammed full of boxes of long-forgotten clutter and multiple cobwebs.

"Absolutely! I could take the blow-up bed in there, and maybe your mum could paint a view on the wall, so it would seem like there was a window!"

"Ah, but there's only one problem," I pointed out to Sandie. "Do you mind sharing?"

"Course not! But who would I have to share with?"

"A couple of hundred spiders!" I grinned.

"Hmm ... maybe I won't," murmured Sandie, crossing her arms over her new PJ top and shuddering. (Sandie hadn't just turned up with new PJs tonight, she'd also been wearing new jeans and trainers. It turned out her mum had taken her out this afternoon for some serious guilt-shopping.)

"Hey, remember the first time you came for a sleepover?" I reminded Sandie, suddenly remembering it myself.

"Oh, yeah! I woke everyone up, didn't I?" Sandie giggled.

She'd had this nightmare that she was drowning, that the air was being crushed out of her as she sank down in some unknown, unnamed sea. She'd woken herself – and me and the rest of the family – with a yell for help. And that yell at close quarters certainly sent poor Colin scampering off on his three legs pretty smartish. I mean, one minute, there he was, happily settling himself down for a snooze on this comfy warm chest, and next thing he was being shoved off and *deafened*...

"And then Rolf woke you up in the morning by wagging his tail in your face!"

"It was like being slapped awake by a furry banana!" Sandie giggled.

"You couldn't get over the amount of pets we had, could you?"

"I couldn't get over the amount of *people* in your house! Not just your dad and Tor and your sisters, but your grandma, and Linn and Rowan's friends. Compared to my house it was like living in Bluewater shopping centre!"

Speaking of Linn's friends...

"Remember the time I told you about how much I fancied Alfie?" I whispered, even though I didn't exactly think Linn would be hovering outside my door, listening in to our late-night conversation. She had better (worse?) things to think about.

"Mmm..." Sandie nodded. "I've never seen anyone go that pink!"

There was lots of secret stuff that I'd told Sandie over the years: stuff about Alfie, but stuff about how much I missed Mum when she wasn't around. And Sandie had listened, and hadn't told me I was an idiot, or that I had a *way* less-than-zero chance of Alfie ever fancying *me*. And she never said dumb, useless things like, "It'll be all right, your mum'll come back," when we didn't know if that would *ever* happen.

And she'd been there on one of the most amazing, dazzlingly brilliant days of my life, when Mum *had* come back. On that day, Sandie had been so deliriously chuffed for me that the memory of it – and everything else about her being my best friend – suddenly made hot tears prickle at my eyes.

"I'm going to miss you, Ally!" Sandie's voice wobbled, as she spotted my watery eyes.

"I'm going to miss you too!" I choked out, as we threw our arms around each other and started sobbing big-time.

And somewhere in my dark bedroom, Rolf – oblivious to us – snuffled and turned over in his sleep, letting out a contented, smelly fart at the same time.

OK, maybe there were one or two things about this house and family that Sandie *wasn't* going to miss...

Chapter 11

(WAY) UNDER BETH'S RADAR

Whenever there's a party, there's always *one* balloon that gets missed out of the post-party tidy-up. That's the balloon that you find behind the sofa a week later, all shrivelled and squishily knobbly.

Got that shrivelled, squishily knobbly rubbery shape in your head?

Good.

Well, now you'll know what I mean when I say that Billy looked like a post-party balloon on Tuesday morning when I went around to see him.

Spookily enough, Sandie had looked a bit like that too, at breakfast earlier, after her sleepover. She'd hardly been able to eat her wholemeal pancakes for moping. At first Mum thought that her new pancake recipe must be lousy,* but then she realized Sandie was just in a fug of total gloom and misery over moving away.

(*Sorry, Mum, but they *were* lousy – they tasted

a bit like soggy cardboard beer mats. Not that I've eaten those too often.)

"*Try* not to be sad, Sandie. Remember: you can come and stay here with us any time you like!" Mum had tried to console her.

Consoling Sandie wasn't the best move; it just made her sadder and she'd started snivelling a bit, which of course made *me* snivel a bit. I guess 'cause Sandie was a guest (and the one moving away), Mum had felt compelled to go and put an arm around *her*, while all *I* got in the way of comfort was Rolf flopping his head into my lap, gazing up at me with his liquid brown eyes, and Tor offering me the half a sausage he had left on his plate. Both were kind gestures, but Rolf kind of ruined it by eating the sausage.

Sandie headed home – well, what was "home" for a few more days, anyway – a little while after that, with Mr Penguin tucked in the crook of her arm. Ivy had insisted that Mr Penguin would help Sandie feel better. (He was on a strictly short-term loan *only*. Although Ivy was the proud co-owner of a jungle of soft toys in her and Tor's bedroom, Mr Penguin was *special*. Well, as special as a ratty, well-worn, well-hugged and well-sucked piece of cloth *can* be...)

And once Sandie had mooched off, I decided I

should head round to Billy's and make sure he was OK/still talking to me/hadn't decided the world was a cruel, cruel place and locked himself in a dark cupboard for eternity.

But walking up to his front door, I could already figure out that he hadn't gone for the dark cupboard option – his upstairs bedroom window was open, Manchester United curtains fluttering gently in the breeze, with the Red Hot Chili Peppers' "Can't Stop" blasting out at top volume, accompanied by loud, repetitive thumps.

I pressed the doorbell, wondering how exactly Billy was going to hear the trilling of it above all the noise coming from his room (one thing was for sure – his mum and dad were out at work, or he wouldn't have *dared* blast the music out so loud). But, surprise, surprise, the door was yanked open almost immediately.

For a second I was flummoxed to find myself looking at a face so much like Billy's, but with a scowl slapped on it instead of a dopey grin. It had probably been a couple of years since I'd set eyes on Beth – she didn't drag herself back from her exciting job as a translator in Paris to see her family too often.

"Oh. Er, hello. Is Billy home?"

It was a dumb question to ask, I guess. It wasn't

as if the ghost of a previous tenant was currently in his room, operating the CD player and pogoing around to the Chili Peppers.

"Ally, hi!" Beth's face suddenly lit up as she recognized me. "Wow, it's been *ages* since I've seen you! You look great! Why don't you come in and we'll have a lovely girly chat over some yummy French cakes I brought over from this brilliant little patisserie I know in Montmartre!"

OK, that's how Beth might have welcomed me in a parallel universe. Instead she stood scowling just inside the doorway, staring dully at me and clutching a magazine. I'd obviously interrupted her reading.

In what felt like excruciating slow motion, she flicked her eyes up and down the length of me, like an anaconda giving a scrawny rabbit the once-over to decide whether it's worth the effort of killing and eating such a pathetic specimen. Or maybe she was just trying to remember who such a nobody actually was, despite having known me since I was about three.

"Oi! Idiot! Someone for you!" she barked sulkily up the stairs.

"Idiot"? Maybe I called Billy a berk, but I was allowed to – I was his mate and hung out with him nearly every day. What gave Beth the right to be so mean when she'd only been back in Britain for five minutes?

Before that thought had swivelled through my brain, Beth had already turned and slouched off towards the living room to continue with her exhausting flick through the pages of *Marie Claire*. She still hadn't said a word to me, or even invited me in, but I came in anyway, shutting the door softly in case any loud clunks irritated her (even more than she was already irritated).

You know, over the years, I'd got used to being blanked by people a few years older than me, and was never particularly bugged by it. (Dad had a name for this; he called it "being under the radar". When Linn's or Rowan's mates acted like I wasn't in the room, I didn't take it personally. It wasn't as if they disliked me; they just didn't notice I existed ... I was under their radar.) So, growing up, whenever I came around to play at Billy's, I totally expected to be blanked by Beth – it would have been weird if she'd acted any other way. But just now, that "blanking" had an extra edge of plain, well, *rudeness* to it.

"And tell him to turn that rubbish down," Beth grunted – presumably at me – without lifting her eyes from her magazine.

As if the she-devil's wish had come true, the music suddenly died, and Billy's door on the first-floor landing flew open. I sprinted like a bat out of hell up the stairs, just in case I was infected by any toxic vibes emanating from Beth.

"There you go!" I panted as I hurried past him into his room, hauling a flimsy cardboard box of biscuits out of my bag and thrusting them at the lanky lump of boy that loosely resembled my friend Billy. "Got them specially!"

"Nah, I'm all right..." he shrugged, collapsing on to his bed, doing the deflated balloon thing.

This was worse than I thought. Not only was he horribly miserable, but he was off his (comfort) food too. *And* he looked flushed and a bit sweaty. As if he'd been pogoing around his room, if I didn't know better (i.e. the thumping I'd heard was more likely to be the sound of him battering his head against the wall).

"You had the music up loud," I pointed out, guessing he must have been drowning his sorrows in his favourite, noisy band.

"Er ... yeah. Well, it was me and Sandie's song. Kind of."

"Can't Stop" was *their* song? Since when? Wow, Sandie – princess of fluffy pop – must really have liked Billy (once upon a time) to agree to having a thumping funk-rock track as the soundtrack to their romance.

"So … you OK?" I asked, flopping down beside Billy and tearing open the box of Jaffa Cakes, just to try and entice him.

Of *course* he wasn't all right. His heart was in pieces and he hadn't even *started* to superglue it together again. Even though he liked hanging out with me, I probably reminded him constantly of Sandie. And now that Sandie was leaving for ever…

"Kind of. Yeah. No. Not really," he shrugged, propping himself upright on the bed with one skinny arm and revolving his faded grey baseball cap around and around his head with the other.

"Thinking about Sandie again?" (Ask a stupid question.)

"Huh-yuhhhhhhhhhhhhhhhh."

That was a yes and a sigh and grunt all at once. I sneaked a look at Billy and wondered what it would take to make him less of a crumpled car-wreck of a boy. It didn't seem like hanging out with Stevie and Hassan yesterday had helped shake him out of his blue moody after all.

I dunno, but maybe, I wondered to myself, *maybe I should think about that mad idea – that thing about fixing him up with Jen or Salma or someone. Try and take his muddled mind off Sandie…*

"*And* my sister's still being a pain," Billy mumbled, absently keeping up with the hat-spinning routine,

I noticed. (He ought to watch that – his whole head could come unscrewed.)

"Well, that's not exactly a surprise," I mumbled sympathetically, after my not-exactly-heart-warming reunion with her just now. "Is she still snorting at you?"

"Uh-huh. And she called me a dork this morning."

"Why?"

"'Cause I sneezed at breakfast."

"That's all?"

"Well, I sneezed – *hard* – into my bowl of cornflakes, and the milk and cornflakes kind of *sprayed* everywhere."

OK, so that was a bit disgusting, but it didn't mean Billy particularly deserved to be called a dork, or be snorted at.

"What *is* her problem?" I asked, feeling a niggle of annoyance. Beth hardly ever bothered visiting her family. You'd think she could make the effort and be vaguely nice, even if she was just faking it. I mean, even Linn and Rowan have moments of being nice to each other, and they live together all the time and drive each other mental. Billy seemed to be annoying Beth just by *existing* (and sneezing).

Before we got a chance to discuss what Beth's problem was (it wouldn't have been a very long conversation anyway – she was suffering from a raging case of obnoxious-itis, that was all), I noticed something: without even realizing what he was doing, Billy's hand had stopped whirling his baseball cap around in that demented way and was now conveying a Jaffa Cake to his mouth.

"Mmm! These are just ace, aren't they?" he mumbled after a mouthful, looking slightly less deflated all of a sudden.

Hey, it wasn't earth-shattering stuff, but it seemed like a positive sign to me. Billy would be all right – I, Ally Love, his best mate, would make sure of it. And if Jaffa Cakes helped him over his ordeal, then how much better would he be if there was a potential new girlfriend on the scene?

And then the spookiest thing happened – I caught Billy sort of staring at me, as if he could read my thoughts. But nah; that rapturous look was probably (definitely) nothing to do with Billy suddenly developing amazing psychic powers and *everything* to do with the joy of Jaffa Cakes...

Chapter 12

MY TOP FIVE NO-FUN LIST

It was nearly quarter to two, and Sandie was late for our girls'-only lunch date. Me and the others had been here for forty-five minutes already, and if we didn't order something soon, I was pretty sure the bored KFC crew working today would be tempted to chuck us out, just to brighten up their dull shift.

Luckily, for Kyra and Chloe and co, I was entertaining them with tales of Beth's obnoxiousness from this morning.

"She didn't even say hello when she saw it was you, even though you've known her family for years?" Jen gasped, wide-eyed (i.e. her doll-sized eyes almost looked as big as normal people's for a change).

"Not a hello, not anything. She just stared at me as if I was a particularly repulsive slug."

It had been three hours since that slug-hating stare, and the thought of it still made me shudder. Poor Billy having to live with that cloud of poisonous gas for however long Beth decided to stay (which she hadn't decided yet, apparently).

"Hey, here comes Sandie now!" Kellie pointed out of the window.

All of us peered through the plate glass at her, sending beams of sympathy her way. The others already knew Sandie's news, but this was the first time they'd seen her and I suspected she was about to be smothered in hugs the second she came in here.

"Um, Ally ... I thought you said she was really, really upset at the moment?" Chloe muttered dubiously, her dark red eyebrows practically slamming into each other as she frowned.

"Yeah! She's looking a bit, well, *happy* for someone who's supposed to be sad!" Kyra mumbled, joining Chloe in the frowning game.

They were right. There was Sandie, practically *skipping* across the road as the green man bleeped, waving cheerfully at the bus driver who'd reluctantly screeched his no. 91 bus to a halt at the traffic lights. With her blonde ponytail flipping out behind her, she looked like she was in some corny ad for sanitary towels or something. ("I can have fun – no matter *what* time of the month it is, thanks to wings!")

I tried to open my mouth, to describe how

gloomy and blue Sandie had been when she (and Mr Penguin) had left my place this morning, but I couldn't quite match up that miserable person at breakfast time to the positively shiny, happy person bounding towards the KFC and us.

"Hi, everyone!" Sandie called out, scurrying through the door and over to join us, and plopping her bag on the table before she sat herself down in the one free seat we'd kept for her.

"Ooh! *Nice* bag!" Kellie drooled, stroking the felt flowers and beads stitched on it.

"Mum bought it for me this morning as a surprise. Gorgeous, isn't it?"

Er … hello? Was this Sandie's bright and bubbly identical twin sister? Where was the girl who left my house this morning? The girl who didn't much want to talk to her mum at the moment, the girl who looked like she'd never smile again any time soon?

"Where've you been? You're really late!" I asked this alien Sandie instead.

I think that *might* just have come out sounding a little snippy; Chloe certainly shot me a quick what's-with-the-attitude? look. But I couldn't help it – I was confused (i.e. more confused than normal).

"Sorry! Jacob phoned me just as I was about to

leave the house," Sandie babbled excitedly.

"Oh, yeah – he's coming to London to see you tomorrow, isn't he?" Jen grinned. "Are you excited?"

"Definitely!" Sandie giggled shyly. "I can't wait!"

She smiled my way specifically, and then I remembered that I was supposed to hang out with the lovebirds. She'd started speaking about Jacob and the day out last night, but we'd got sidetracked by our slushily sad meander down memory lane...

"But hold on – what about you moving away, Sand? We can't *believe* that's happening!"

That was Salma, getting back to the main issue of the day after everyone had got temporarily distracted by Sandie's big smile and fancy new bag.

"And I can't believe my parents are *doing* that to me!" Sandie shrugged hopelessly. But weirdly enough, the smile on her face didn't seem to fade too much.

And then – when she came out with what she came out with next – I suddenly understood *why*.

"But the brilliant thing is, when we were talking just now, Jacob pointed out that we'll be living really close to each other! I didn't realize that Bath was so near Bristol – it's only a half-hour drive away!"

Well, thank goodness our geography teacher had just gone off on maternity leave, or she might well have gone into premature labour at the shock of finding out how little Sandie knew about the geography of Britain...

"Wow!"

"Ooh, Sandie – that's great!"

"That means you'll be able to see him practically *all* the time!"

"Lucky you!"

They were cooing: all my mates were actually *cooing*. OK, maybe not Kyra, but she was still managing to look well chuffed for Sandie. So why wasn't I cooing or looking well chuffed for my best mate?

Maybe it was because I felt... How exactly did I feel? Hurt? Let down? Betrayed, even? It was something to do with the fact that me and Sandie had spent last night and this morning talking and blubbing and missing each other already, and now here she was just a few hours later; all bubbly and bright and excited about the move, just because Jacob the Wonderful mattered more to her than ... well, *me*.

Good grief – now I had more in common with Billy than just a love of nachos, Ben & Jerry's ice-cream and talking rubbish. Now we were both totally jealous of the same boy for taking Sandie away from us.

"Oh, Ally, before I forget!" Sandie suddenly

announced, rifling in the depths of her oversized, slouchy new bag. "Can you give this back to Ivy? I don't need it any more!"

Yanking Mr Penguin out by the neck, she plonked him in front of me on the table, not realizing she'd aimed straight for a stray blob of ketchup. With his stuffed head lolling to one side, he looked totally forlorn.

I know how you feel, I told him silently in my head.

School holidays are meant to be like heaven, aren't they? Well, from a fun point of view, this week was turning out to be less like heaven and more like a trip to the dentist.

Once I'd checked out of the KFC and left my mates to it ("to it" meaning listening to Sandie twitter on about how fantastic moving to Bath was going to be), I aimlessly wandered around some shops on Crouch End Broadway, mentally racking up a No-Fun List. It went like this...

<u>My Top Five No-Fun List</u>
1) Billy languishing in the pits of gloom over the break-up with Sandie.

2) The shock of Sandie moving away.

3) Sandie languishing in the pits of gloom over moving away. (Or maybe not.)

4) The shock of Linn planning on moving away.

5) Linn languishing in the pits of gloom 'cause she can't move away.

And if that lot wasn't enough, I had that whole weird vibe that I couldn't quite shake off. Maybe I was just unsettled or something. I mean, one minute I was feeling horribly sorry for Sandie, and the next minute I was mad at her for cheering up about the whole move thing. And one minute Billy's clinginess was driving me insane, and the next minute I felt like putting my arms around the big berk and giving him a sympathetic hug.

It was all doing my head in. Why couldn't this just be a normal shopping/lazing/hanging out kind of half-term holiday? Please?

Anyway, speaking of the three people helping make my week a no-fun zone, here I was outside Seasons; the clothes shop Linn works in on Saturdays and during the holidays. And there was Linn, standing by the till, staring a hole through the glass-top counter.

"Busy, then?" I tried to joke, poking my head around the door.

"It's non-stop!" Linn said wryly, lifting her gaze to meet mine and thankfully looking sort of pleased to see me.

"Is it OK if I come in for a minute? I don't want to distract you from your customers!" I said, wafting my arm around the completely empty shop.

"I think that would be all right," she smiled, folding her arms across the front of her crisp white shirt. "So … what's up?"

What was up was that I really wanted to ask her how she felt about the whole Edinburgh thing, but with Linn, you have to tread kind of carefully. You could ask Rowan the most personal questions, and she'd just *blah* out an answer without thinking; but Linn … Linn is an expert at taking offence easily, or just shutting up and locking all her secrets up inside if she thinks that you're noseying or meddling. So instead of asking her what I wanted to ask her, I babbled about something totally different instead.

"Just wondered what you're getting for Tor's birthday on Saturday. Just so we don't buy him the same thing."

"I haven't decided yet," Linn shrugged. "Been a bit busy thinking about other stuff. Why – do you know what you're buying for him?"

"Uh, yeah – I think so. It's a dog bowl. With ears."

I know it might seem strange to give your kid brother a present that's really not for him, but Tor's so animal-mental that he'd appreciate a pet-related pressie more than anything. And anyway, there was always a chance that he'd eat out of it himself...

"OK, so I won't get him one of those, then!" Linn laughed.

Oh, good, she laughed. I liked that. Maybe she wasn't feeling so bad about Edinburgh after all. But maybe I should just check.

"So ... with the dental school thingummy," I began warily, hoping I wasn't going to bug her. "Are you going to apply to one in London now?"

"I s'pose so," Linn answered flatly, her laugh instantly evaporating. "Alfie will be pleased, 'cause he's sticking around London. I'll miss Mary and Nadia, though – they're both going to Edinburgh."

Now it was Linn's turn to look like a half-deflated balloon. It was as if the very mention of Edinburgh had sucked all the happiness right out of her.

"I'm glad you're not going. I don't want you to leave home," I told Linn bluntly, hoping that might cheer her up.

Well, it was true – I didn't want her to leave home, even if it was what Linn wanted more than anything. All of a sudden I couldn't help panicking that she would end up like Beth, having too much of a good time far, far away that she hardly ever came back to see us, and was grumpy and miserable when she did...

"Thanks, that's nice of you to say, Ally," she said, forcing a smile on her face.

But then I suppose what I'd said was only *half* true – I wasn't so selfish that I wanted to watch Linn forcing smiles on her face while two of her best mates flounced off to Scotland without her.

What a totally yuck situation. I just wished there was something I could do to cheer her up, but I couldn't think of one, single, solitary thing. Or could I?

"Urgh! What's happened to *him*?" Linn suddenly grimaced at the skanky object I was holding out to her.

Ah, well maybe not.

Linn might be unhappy, but she was still a neat-freak at heart, and so Mr Penguin probably *wasn't* the best bet to comfort her, seeing as he was well tatty and in *serious* need of a trip around the washing machine...

Chapter 13

BLEURRRGGHHHHH...

"If you feel nauseous at any time," the anonymous voice had boomed over the tannoy before the movie started, *"just close your eyes for a moment or two and the feeling should leave you."*

The warning had seemed funny. But then the four of us had the giggles *anyway*, just 'cause we all looked so drop-dead stupid in our matching, geeky 3D specs.

But it wasn't so funny once I started watching the three-dimensional ship getting chucked around in the three-dimensional storm. I tried closing my eyes "for a moment or two", and then opened them – and *still* felt sick. For the whole hour that me, Salma, Sandie and Jacob watched the exploration of the wreck of the *Titanic*, I felt as travel-sick/3D-sick/plain *sick*-sick as I ever had in my whole life. I wished I'd never agreed to come to this stupid movie; I wished I'd stayed safely at home, making toilet-roll animals for Tor's stall at the school fête on Saturday along with Tor, Mum and Rowan.

"Y'know, Ally," Jacob had said, when he saw me struggling not to hurl, "I heard that if you run cold water on your wrists for a bit, *that* can stop you feeling sick!"

It's hard to stay annoyed with someone if they're being really nice to you. And that was the problem with Jacob – he was pretty all-round nice. Nice, kind, funny, smart, tall, cute-looking... How could I even stay mad at Sandie for being delirious at the idea of moving closer to him and being able to see this nice, kind, funny, smart, tall, cute-looking boy more often?

"Is the cold water working?" asked Salma, her perky bum parked on the sink beside me.

"I think so," I murmured, now that the hurling sensation seemed to be slipping away. I wished it would hurry up and slip away completely, so that I could take my frozen wrists out from under the torrent of cold water currently battering out of the tap. I was *sure* I was getting weird looks from people wandering in and out of the Science Museum loos. They'd come in and I'd have my hands in the sink; then they'd come out of the cubicle and I'd *still* have my hands in the sink. They must have thought I was a total oddball, like one of those obsessive/compulsive types who have to wash their hands fifty thousand times an hour or something.

"Well, don't worry about it. Sandie didn't feel too good either," Salma said comfortingly. But I could tell she was a bit bored hanging around and nursemaiding me. I could tell by the way she was examining her long, dark hair for split ends.

"You can go and hang out with her and Jacob outside if you like," I offered her.

Sandie hadn't felt quite as pukey as me – she'd reckoned that a few gulps of fresh air would sort her out.

"Nah, it's OK – I'll leave them on their own," Salma shrugged, and then started nibbling an offending split end off.

And then I decided, now that I had Salma to myself, I might as well go for it; I might as well give the whole isn't-Billy-brilliant? thing a go. Hadn't I decided on this yesterday? Wasn't this the point of me phoning and asking Salma along today? (Yeah, that and the fact that I didn't want to be number three in the two's-company-three's-a-crowd equation when it came to Sandie and Jacob.)

So I'd chosen Salma. How come? Well, I'd already narrowed the field down to her and Jen, so last night in bed, while I was waiting for sleep and the not-quite-kissing dream, I'd passed the time by running over their suitability in detail. (For example: JEN – sweet, funny, giggly. But sometimes annoyingly giggly. SALMA – gorgeous. Super-cool. But sometimes so gorgeous and super-cool that you feel about as attractive as a turnip in her presence.)

After weighing up all their pros and cons for ages, I finally settled on playing "One potato, two potato" and ended up with Salma. And now here she was, examining her split ends and up for a chat to fill the time while I got my heaving stomach under control.

"Billy would have loved that movie!" I exclaimed, as I began my attempt to drop his wondrousness into the conversation.

"No, he wouldn't," Salma contradicted me, without lifting her eyes from her hair-by-hair examination. "Not if he'd had to sit right next to Sandie and her new boyfriend!"

Er, true.

OK, I needed to say something else quick … something that might help me figure out if there was the faintest, tiniest chance of Salma liking Billy *that* way.

"Jacob's great, isn't he?" I said, coming at the Billy subject from a different angle.

"Yeah, he is really great," Salma nodded, raising up her perfectly arched eyebrows enthusiastically.

"He's pretty funny. Like when he was goofing

and asking the guy collecting the 3D glasses if he could keep a pair 'cause they were so cool."

"Yeah, that *was* pretty funny," Salma grinned at the memory of the flustered attendant, who didn't know if he was getting the mickey taken out of him or not. (He was.)

"But he's not as funny as Billy, is he? Could you imagine if it had been *Billy* here today instead of Jacob?" I suggested. "That would have been *mad*!"

"Yeah, he'd have probably made up stupid sound effects or something!" Salma laughed, raising her head and looking at me instead of her split ends for once. "Or bet you he'd have shouted out 'Boo!' when the camera was going along all those spooky empty corridors in the *Titanic*!"

This was good; the mention of Billy seemed to have really got her attention.

"Yeah, he would have, wouldn't he?" I giggled encouragingly. "Y'know, I do *like* Jacob, but Billy's so funny and everything, you wonder how come Sandie could have chucked him sometimes, don't you?"

"Are you *kidding*, Ally?" Salma raised those eyebrows of hers up, up and away. "I mean, Billy's brilliant, but come on – he's a bit of a *doughball*. And Jacob – he's absolutely *gorgeous*! I'm telling you, if *I'd* been on that geography trip and seen him first…"

Grrrrrr.

Maybe I shouldn't have played that game of "One potato, two potato" yesterday. Maybe if I'd done something more scientific like picking one of their names out of a hat, I'd have *Jen* here with me today.

Something told me she'd be a *much* nicer potential girlfriend for "doughball" Billy...

Chapter 14

TWO STEGOSAURUSES, COMING THROUGH!

All the way home from the Science Museum, I'd felt pretty bugged at Salma for calling Billy a doughball.

Then I got back home and found him sitting on the floor of our living room, practically covered in toilet paper.

In fact, Billy was *so* mummified that the only way I knew it was him was because the peak of his baseball cap was sticking out through the layers upon layers of loo roll.

"Ivy?" his muffled voice mumbled from behind the recycled paper.

"Nope. It's Ally."

"Oh, hi, Ally!" he said brightly, ripping one hand up through the reams of loo roll and tearing a hole round about where his eyes were. The only problem was, his aim was slightly wrong, and all I found myself staring at was a bit of one eye and most of Billy's nose.

What a doughball...

"Er … *why?*" I asked him pointedly, sticking my hands on my hips and staring down at him.

Billy blinked at me with the half of one eye that was visible.

"It's not Billy's fault," said Grandma, breezing in from the hall. "I asked him to help me out and keep Ivy entertained because your mum's nipped out and Ivy was getting in Tor's way while he was making things for his stall."

Grandma seemed to glance around for signs of my little sister before lowering her voice and carrying on.

"Tor got a bit upset when he caught her glueing a toilet-roll tube to the tortoise," she whispered conspiratorially.

"You mean, to a *cardboard* tortoise, or the real thing?" I whispered back.

By the end of last night, the kitchen table had looked like it contained a Noah's ark worth of toilet-roll tube animals for Tor's school fête stall. (Actually, I don't remember Noah having two stegosauruses on the ark, but maybe I was just off the day they covered that in RE lessons.) By tonight – after another day's worth of frantic toilet-tube modelling – I wondered if we'd even be able to find the kitchen floor under that sea of cardboard pets.

"The *real* one," Grandma replied, pulling a face.

Poor Spartacus. I guess, being a tortoise, he just wasn't as talented in the running-away-fast department as any of our other pets. (With the exception of the stick insects, who never move anyway.)

At that moment, a small pink blur came from nowhere and hurtled past our knees, coming to a stop beside my doughball of a best boy mate.

"Look!" trilled Ivy, twirling on the spot in her pink dungarees and pink-and-white gingham trainers. "A snowman!"

So *that's* what Billy was meant to be.

"And what do snowmen do when the sun comes out, Ivy?" I asked her, walking over to Billy and grabbing the stray end of loo roll that I'd spotted.

"Don't KNOW!" Ivy shouted loudly, for no apparent reason except for the fact that she was only three and a half and didn't know the reason she was shouting loudly herself.

"They melt!" I grinned at her, unravelling lengths of paper and starting to set Billy free.

Uh-oh.

I was trying to be funny, but it looked like Ivy was on the verge of giggling, or bursting into tears. Luckily, Grandma saved the day.

"What about we go out into the garden and let Cilla see your new shoes, Ivy!" she suggested brightly.

"*Yessssss!*" roared Ivy, as though showing off her new trainers to a rabbit was just about the most exciting event since man landed on the moon.

"So…" I turned to Billy, still unravelling him as Ivy and Grandma exited and the room became a calmer and much less pink place to be. "I was, er, at the IMAX cinema at the Science Museum this afternoon."

Urgh! This wasn't fun. I hadn't mentioned the IMAX trip to Billy when I saw him this morning 'cause I thought it was better not to, if you see what I mean. But then I hadn't expected him to drop by like he had and force me to come clean.

"Yeah, I know. With Sandie and her new boyfriend. Your grandma told me."

Billy was staring straight at me, and I found that I couldn't stare straight back at him; it was somehow too weird. OK, I was wracked with guilt, I suppose. Then *Billy* went weird, dropping his gaze to the floor as his cheeks flushed pink. Uh-oh – was he gearing up to ask me for details about Sandie and Jacob? What could I say? Tell him how great they were getting on and make him truly miserable? Or fib for his sake and tell him they were about as compatible as a fish and a bicycle?

"Yoooo-hoooo! Anybody want to hear my brilliant news?" Mum's voice drifted in from the front door, rescuing me from an awkward moment with Billy.

Well, it looked like quite a few people wanted to hear Mum's great news: me, Billy, Tor and Ivy practically collided with her in the hall, while Grandma strolled more sedately out of the kitchen carrying a semi-finished toilet-roll tube sheep, and Rowan appeared on the first-floor landing, her two fat braids dangling as she leant over the bannister to see what was going on.

"I ... Melanie Love ... your mother..." Mum began, spreading her arms out wide (which was only a little bit wider than the huge smile on her face), "have got..."

"Ice-cream! Hurray!" Ivy squealed, bouncing up and down on the spot, clapping her hands.

"Er ... *no*, not ice-cream," Mum laughed, realizing that her dramatic pauses didn't really work for Ivy.

"Toys!" Ivy babbled instead.

"No, no ... wait, sweetie, and I'll tell you!" Mum laughed again, reaching down and scooping Ivy up. "Listen – I've got a job!"

"Oh, that's wonderful, Melanie!" Grandma announced.

You could tell Mum thought it was pretty wonderful too, from the way her eyes were twinkling and the way she was dancing around the hall with Ivy in her arms and her hippy Indian skirt fanning out all around her.

"Yeah!" Tor shouted, taking over from Ivy in the bouncing up and down and hand-clapping department. "Mum's got a job!"

"Mum's got a job!" I repeated happily, infected by his sweet bounciness.

"Mum's going to earn lots and lots of money!" he shouted out, bouncing like an out-of-control Tigger.

"Er ... I wouldn't say *that*, exactly, Tor!" Mum grinned, still spinning and swirling. "It's only teaching art classes to kids on a Saturday morning!"

"But it's brilliant, Mum!" Tor gushed, hurtling himself forward and happily hugging her legs, instantly putting a stop to her spinning.

Um, OK ... he was getting a bit over-the-top now.

"Well, I'm glad you're so pleased, honey!" Mum told the top of Tor's head. She was still smiling, but frowning a little bit too.

"Yay! We're not going to be poor any more!" yelped Tor some more. "So that means that Linn can go away to Edinburgh now, can't she, Mum?"

Oops.

Funny how quickly a brilliant atmosphere can go flat as a pancake…

While Tor had been in the kitchen making more of his cardboard animals this afternoon, Rowan had been busy in her room, making her own floral contribution to Saturday's stall.

"Poor Tor…" I mumbled, clearing a bum-sized space in the mountain of pink and red tissue-paper roses spread over Rowan's bed.

(I had to do a double-take before I sat down; and then I realized that the roses I could still see were just the ones printed on her white duvet cover.)

"I know. Poor little guy," Rowan agreed, lighting the first of her sequinned candles on the Johnny Depp shrine.

Tor had been so upset when Mum and Grandma had tried to gently explain the economics of Mum's Saturday morning job versus the cost of four years' living and studying in an expensive city. In fact, he'd been so upset that the only thing Mum could think of doing to vaguely cheer him up was offer to walk round with the dogs and meet Dad from work. That's where Mum, Tor, Ivy, Rolf, Winslet and Ben were just now (*boy*, was Dad going to get a surprise at the size of his home-time escort).

Meanwhile, doughball Billy had headed back to his house, and the joy of a family meal with his mum, dad, "lovely" Beth and some assorted auntie/uncle types, and Grandma had hurried back to the calm of her own peaceful flat, which contained only one well-behaved pensioner (Stanley) and a very clean, minimally furry cat (Mushu). There was no sign of Linn coming home from work yet, so in a moment of unaccustomed emptiness in our normally packed house, I'd found myself barging in on Ro.

"And then there's Linn, course. I spoke to her today – I went in to see her at the shop," I told Rowan, as I picked up one tissue-paper rose and twirled it back and forth in my fingers. "She's really down about the whole Edinburgh thing."

Rowan seemed to be examining the roses too. She bent over and plucked a bundle off the bed, and began artistically dotting them around her shrine.

"Yeah, I told Alfie he was being an idiot today," she murmured, stepping back and studying the layout of her shrine.

"About Johnny Depp?" I asked, a bit confused and bemused.

"Yeah, that – *and* the fact that he wants Linn to study in London, just 'cause that's what *he's* going to do. I told him that he shouldn't be so selfish!"

Well done to Rowan for standing up for Linn, specially when Linn didn't often come down on Rowan's side. (Did I say often? I probably meant *ever*.)

"I wish there *was* a way Linn could go to Edinburgh," I sighed.

"Mmm," mumbled Ro, scooping an armful of roses up off the bed this time, and starting to dot them around the shrine in big, bold clusters.

"But there's no way that can happen, is there? Not without some fairy godmother appearing out of nowhere!"

"Mmm…"

Ro's pile of stall-bound roses was disappearing fast, as she grabbed more and more of them and started bunching them up in every tiny gap between framed photos and candles and daft-doll statuettes.

"Are you listening to me?"

"Mmm…"

OK, so she wasn't.

"Did you know that Colin's planning on opening a shop specially for three-legged cats?" I babbled, waiting for a reaction. "He's going to sell mini cat-skateboards, so that three-leggers can zoom along the garden just as fast as your average cat."

"Mmm…"

Rowan's great, but the thing about her is, you

have to remember that her head is mostly stuffed full of fluff and glitter, and when *that* side of her brain clicks in, you've just got to shrug and give her up to the lure of pretty colours and shiny surfaces.

"See you later, then," I told her, slipping off her bed and heading towards the door. "I'm just going to go and meet Johnny Depp to do a tandem parascending glide off the top of Ally Pally!"

"Mmm…"

Flowers and candles and sequins and fluff. Sometimes I wished I could live in Rowan's brain instead of my own – it seemed like it was a lot more twinkly and relaxing in there than my own stupid, stress-filled twisty head…

Chapter 15

ANYONE FOR A GAME OF "PUSSYDOG"?

"Ally? Are you still there?"

"Uh, yeah. Sorry," I apologized to Billy, slightly distracted from our Thursday morning phone conversation.

The reason I was momentarily distracted was because Ben was smiling at me. It's kind of nice but also kind of *freaky* having a dog just sit and stare and smile straight at you.

And Ivy was standing right beside Ben, staring hard at me too (but *not* smiling), while cuddling (OK, *gripping*) a cat that wasn't Colin in her arms. I think the cat had realized that wriggling and struggling was a waste of time, and had decided to try another tactic to escape. It (Eddie, by the look of those fight-chewed ears) had gone totally limp, like a soggy rag doll. This was pretty smart of Eddie; his dead weight was making him slither nicely out of Ivy's grasp. Still with her eyes locked on me, Ivy tried to haul Eddie back into place, but he kept right on slithering slowly towards freedom.

"Ally!" she announced suddenly. "Come and play 'pussydog'!"

I had no idea what "pussydog" was, but I was kind of hoping someone else would play it with Ivy, seeing as I was busy.

"Ivy, I'm on the phone to Billy," I told her gently.

Ivy studied me hard, then decided that was no excuse.

"Bye, bye, Billy! Ally, come and play 'pussydog'!"

"OK! OK! In a minute!" I tried to pacify her. "You go and, er … start first!"

Floop. (That was Eddie, slumping on to the floor. Before anyone could blink – never mind think – he'd sprung back to his full catty powers and bolted for the garden, cleverly avoiding being dragged into a game of "pussydog", whatever that was…)

"Eddie*eeeeeeeeeee*!" Ivy called out forlornly, before hurtling off in hot pursuit, with Ben bringing up the rear with some top-volume barking.

"Just another normal day at the Love zoo?" Billy joked, once the mayhem had died away.

"You got it!" I grinned back, getting a buzz from hearing yet another little glimmer of the old, dopey Billy filtering through the bleak blue mood he'd been bogged down in for so long now. "So what about you? How's life at the Stevenson residence?"

"Boring. As usual. Beth's still snorting at me."

"Stupid moo. So, do you want to come on over, or meet up in the park or something?" I suggested. I wasn't seeing Sandie till later in the day (there was a packing frenzy going on at her place right now).

"Yeah. I mean, well, Stevie just phoned and said that the lads are going to hang out at the half-pipe again today, but I didn't fancy it."

The skateboard park that the council had built was basically one wooden ramp they'd squeezed into a tea-towel-sized space in-between the entrance to the skating rink at Ally Pally and the kids' play area. But even if it wasn't very big or flash, all the skateboarders from Crouch End and Muswell Hill flocked there (well, it was still better than skating along boring pavements and running into irate old grannies and getting shouted at).

And whether Billy fancied it or not, he *was* going to the skateboard park today. Like Kyra had said, him hanging out with his mates was practically *medicinal* in the circumstances.

"Hey, I'd love to go!" I lied enthusiastically. "I love watching you guys do your stunts!"

Ha! I loved seeing them crashing when they tried to do their stunts, more like.

"Yeah, you sure, Al?" said Billy, sounding dead chuffed for some reason. "You wouldn't be bored?"

Nope, I wouldn't be bored, 'cause I didn't plan

on hanging around watching on my *own*. Oh yes ...
I might even manage to do some subtle match-
making at the same time as watching boys fall off
their skateboards.

"I'll be fine. So when are we going up there?" I
asked Billy, while I flicked through the address book
on the hall table and stopped at "H" for Hudson...

"I saw Kyra in the library yesterday afternoon."

"*Kyra*? The *library*?" I frowned, thinking Jen
had gone mad or something. No *way* would Kyra
willingly hang out in a library, unless it was the
school one and she was there doing detention.

"That telly crew were filming just outside it,"
Jen went on to explain. "Kyra was inside, sitting
beside a window with a book."

OK, so that made more sense. Kyra was
obviously still stalking the programme makers.

"Do you think she managed to get in the
shot, then?"

"Nah. She wasn't very pleased when I went over
to talk to her and pointed out that the cameras
were facing *away* from the library, not *towards* it."

"What book was she pretending to read
anyway?" I asked, curious to imagine Kyra holding
one in her hands. Books were so alien to her that it
was a wonder she knew how to turn the pages.

"Wait for this – something about prostate trouble for men!" Jen grinned. "She must have just grabbed it without looking!"

"No!" I gasped and giggled at the same time.

Thunk!

"Oooof!" me and Jen both winced together, glancing round in the direction of the ominous *thunk*ing noise.

A small kid had just done an impressive swoop from the top of the half-pipe and then parted company with his board somewhere in mid-air. Luckily for the board (and unfortunately for the kid), its fall was broken by the kid's head.

Ouch.

"That's *got* to have hurt," I mumbled, as I watched Billy, Hassan and a couple of other lads run over and check on the splatted kid.

"Is he *dead*?" Jen fretted, slapping her hands across her face and barely bringing herself to peek through her fingers.

"Nah – look, he's OK," I told her, watching the bigger lads help the stunned younger boy to his (wobbly) feet. Anyway, Billy was looking over and giving me the thumbs-up, so it seemed like the little guy was only suffering a large dent to his pride (and *maybe* a mild concussion).

"Aww … that's really nice of Billy and Hassan to

help him out, isn't it?" Jen noted, now that she was reassured enough to drop her hands from her face and watch what was going on.

Perfect! Jen was impressed by Billy! Why didn't I pick *her* as his potential new girlfriend in the first place, instead of pinning my hopes on Salma yesterday? Doh!

Anyway, as we kept on watching, Mr Impressive (i.e. Billy) started leading the kid over towards a bench to rest up, while Hassan carried over the killer board. Meanwhile, Stevie and Richie/Ricardo (Billy's big-headed, small-brained mate), were both standing eating Snickers bars and uninterestedly keeping an eye on the whole trauma like it was something off the telly.

And speaking of the telly...

"Hey, look, Ally! That's one of those big location vans, isn't it?" Jen pointed out, as a large white truck with "Artist Services" written on the side trundled slowly past us and turned right into the car park. "I wonder what's in there?"

"I think it's the lunch lorry," I told her, dispelling any ideas she might have of the truck being packed with cutting-edge, state-of-the-art camera equipment (it was full of burgers – Mum had seen it when it was parked outside Ivy's nursery).

"Oh..." mumbled Jen, looking faintly

disappointed. (Maybe she'd even been hoping that the back doors of the truck would open up and a bundle of super-famous actors would come spilling out or something.)

"If the lunch lorry's here, they must be filming around the Palace somewhere," I told her. "How about when Billy and the boys are finished here, we could all go and have a nosey around and see if we can spot the TV crew? Or even see if we can spot Kyra hiding in the bushes?"

"Yeah! Let's!" sniggered Jen. "Better watch Billy, though – you know what he's like! He'll *definitely* wangle into the background and do something dumb like make bunny-ears behind the main actor!"

Hurrah! Jen was mentioning Billy again! Without any prompting from me! And she thought he was funny! *Yessss!*

"He probably would, wouldn't he?" I grinned. "He's such an idiot – I mean, a laugh!"

Careful – I was supposed to be bigging Billy up right now, not showing him up as the muppet he can be.

"So how's Billy doing anyway? Is he *still* upset about Sandie chucking him?"

Ooh, this seemed like *serious* interest coming from Jen. Didn't it?

"Nah, I think he's pretty much over it," I lied.

"You know how it is – it's like that kid who fell off his skateboard; it's just his pride that got hurt."

"So what does Billy think about her leaving London? Has he spoken to her about it?"

"No … they haven't spoken since they broke up," I explained to Jen, not even bothering to recount that awkward meeting in the park last Sunday morning, since it would involve mentioning the fact that Billy had a dog on his head and that really *would* make him seem like a muppet.

"They still haven't *spoken*?" Jen said in genuine surprise.

I guess I could see why she was so surprised. If Jen could manage to forgive her dad and start talking to him again (after him leaving her and her mum and sister a few weeks ago), then it did seem pretty nuts that Billy and Sandie hadn't got over it and sorted stuff out.

"But she's moving away in two days' time, Ally!" Jen frowned at me, all concerned. "Billy *should* see her, just so there's no hard feelings between them before she goes!"

OK, so Jen was a bit sensitive about people falling out/making up with each other at the moment, but was there more to it than that? It was just that Jen *really* seemed to care…

"S'pose you're right," I shrugged. "I guess it

would be good for them both, specially Billy. But I've tried to get them together before and they both say they're too shy to meet up."

"So? They just need a hand to make it happen, don't they?"

"Do they?" I said, feeling all of a sudden odd about the idea. What if they started arguing or something? Or what if they got back *together*? That was even weirder and gave me goosebumps at the very thought, if you want to know the truth. I mean, I hadn't even considered that – and it would be a terrible thing to happen, wouldn't it? It's like his heart would get squashed even more when she moved away at the weekend. No, no, no … Billy *mustn't* get back with Sandie. He had to fall for Jen, didn't he?

"Hey – maybe you could invite him along to Chloe's tomorrow night!" Jen suggested.

We were having our very last Girls' Video Night together. Well, at least the very last one before Sandie headed off into the West…

"Billy wouldn't come along to that," I shook my head. "He's scared enough of the idea of seeing Sandie, but he'd *die* if all of us were there, just *gawping*."

While Jen blinked her black button eyes and let her brain whirl around in search of possible plans and schemes, I sneaked a sideways peek at her, and wondered if Jen really was The One; The One who could prove to Billy that there was life after Sandie...

"Hey!"

Yikes – I nearly jumped out of my skin at the sound of Billy's voice so unexpectedly close.

Please don't let Billy have heard us talking about him... Please don't let Billy have heard us talking about him...

"Did you see that woman and that guy who were talking to me and the lads just now?" Billy babbled on excitedly, oblivious to the fact that me and Jen were both pink-cheeked and silent in his presence.

"Er ... nope," I shook my head, then glanced around and spotted a couple – both armed with clipboards – making their way towards the lunch lorry.

"They *only* work for the TV company!" Billy gushed.

Well, I'd hope so, or they were about to get burgers under false pretences by the look of it. But why was Billy suddenly so impressed? The TV people had been hovering around Ally Pally and Crouch End for days and days now and Billy hadn't been particularly wowed by them up till now. So what was the big deal?

"You'll never guess what, Ally!"

Billy's eyes were manically wide under the peak of his baseball cap. Any wider and he'd be in danger of his eyeballs popping out.

"What?"

"They're going to be shooting a scene *right* here on Saturday afternoon –"

He pointed to a bit of tarmac about ten centimetres from the tip of my trainer, as if there was a giant x-marks-the-spot spray-painted on there. (There wasn't, by the way.)

"– and they just asked me and Hassan and Stevie and Richie to be extras!"

"Extras!" squeaked Jen, all impressed. "What'll you have to do, Billy?" she quizzed him, looking mildly star-struck herself, now that she was in the presence of a soon-to-be celeb (fnar!).

"Just skateboard in the background! And we get paid and everything! *And* they'll feed us!"

"God, don't tell Kyra – she'll be grabbing a board and buying herself a pair of skater shorts if she finds out!" I laughed, confusing Billy, who didn't know what I was on about.

It was a miracle. Apart from the mild confusion currently splattered on his face, this overexcited streak of daft, lanky boy was definitely looking like the old-skool Billy I knew so well. He was back, back, back (hopefully), thanks to this corny detective programme! Now if I could just get him to fall for Jen, everything would be just about wonderful. Wouldn't it?

"You'll come and see me getting filmed on Saturday, won't you, Ally?" he grinned at me.

"Yeah, like I'd *dare* to miss your starring moment!" I grinned back at him, and then remembered that I'd completely forgotten something. "Oh … but I can't! I already promised to help out at Tor's school fête, and then it's his birthday party…"

"I'll come!" Jen jumped in and offered.

I should have been glad about that – it fitted in to my match-making plans perfectly. But Billy was giving me that sad, stray puppy stare again, making me feel like I was Cruella De Vil instead of his guardian angel…

Chapter 16

STICKING UP FOR THE DOUGHBALL

"Blue again?" I asked, staring down at Billy as he lay sprawled in the watery sunshine in his garden.

"Uh-huh," he muttered soulfully, his face virtually hidden under his baseball cap.

What a difference a few hours can make. Yesterday afternoon – after him and his mates had been asked to "star" in the telly programme – he was nearly back to the daft-as-a-frog, enthusiastic Billy I knew so well. But this Friday morning, it seemed that he was residing in that old pit of gloom again.

"Do you just want some time on your own?" I suggested.

Actually, I was pretty keen to zoom off – I'd only dropped by, while walking the dogs at Ally Pally, to ask him to come out and help me shop for Tor's birthday present in Crouch End this afternoon. I didn't really want him staring at me in that spooky, slightly *psychic* way he'd done a couple of times recently, making me feel like he could see into my thoughts and know I was aiming to set him up with Jen.

"No! Don't go!" he stunned me by yelping, sitting bolt upright and shoving his cap so far back that it took a nosedive straight off the back of his head.

I might have been slightly freaked at his reaction, but a sudden familiar yelping of a different sort distracted us both (not to mention three previously pleasantly snoozling dogs of mine).

"*Yap-yappity-yappity-yappity-yappity-yap-yap-yap!*"

"That'll be Mum and Beth – they just took Precious for a walk," Billy muttered, glancing around at the back gate of the garden, which led directly out on to a lane.

Rolf, Winslet and Ben were all staring expectantly at the gate too. One of them – Winslet, I suspected – was letting out a low growl (and I couldn't blame her).

"*Yap-yappity-yappity-yappity-yappity-yap-yap-yap!*"

Billy's mum's head appeared first, hovering disembodied above the tall, wooden gate, as she rattled and pushed against its stiffness (it didn't budge). Beside her, Beth's face looked blank and bored, as if she was busily daydreaming of this duty-visit home being over. While Beth broke out into a yawn and Mrs Stevenson struggled with the stubborn gate, Precious did the poodle version of the limbo and wriggled his wiry white body under the bottom of the gate, rushing over to my trio of pooches with an excited, *"Yap-yappity-yappity-yappity-yappity-yap-yap-yap!"* as if he expected them and their eardrums to be happy to see and hear him. (How wrong can a dopey dog be?)

"Oh, Billy! You're there!" Mrs Stevenson called out, suddenly spotting her son and me messing up the tidiness of her immaculate lawn. "This gate's sticking again. Can you give it a push from your side?"

As Billy unravelled his long, lanky legs and stood up, I *swear* I saw Beth rolling her eyes, as if even him just doing *that* much irritated her.

And so Billy bounded over, pushed the stubborn wood with his hands, and nothing happened (Beth tutted). Then he put his shoulder against it and gave it a shove, and *still* nothing happened (Beth snorted).

"Isn't it moving, Billy?" Mrs Stevenson frowned at him. "Well, don't worry dear, we'll just come around the front. I'll get your dad to fix it at the weeken— *oh!*"

I don't know whether Billy suddenly kicked at the gate as a last resort to get it open, or if he was maybe just imagining that it was Beth's *head* or something. But whatever, I don't think he'd expected the gate to stay stuck while his trainer crashed through the rotten wooden slats.

At the sound of the ominous *crunch!* and the sight of Billy's one stuck leg wedged amongst the splinters, Precious went into a manic, bouncing-on-the-spot, yappity-yapping frenzy. Mrs Stevenson, meanwhile, had her mouth fixed in a big, surprised "O" shape, as if someone had just pinched her bum and she'd frozen in shock. And Beth? Well, Beth managed to roll her eyes, tut and snort, "Jeez! You *dork*!" all at once.

And somehow ...

that ...

just ...

made ...

me ...

FURIOUS!

"Look! D'you want to SHUT UP and stop giving Billy a hard time for five minutes, Beth?"

Oh, yes. For three whole seconds, I felt so protective of Billy that I'd turned into the Crouch End version of The Hulk (only slightly less muscly and green). Amazingly, I didn't care *what* I said or *who* heard.

By the *fourth* second, I suddenly remembered that I was only 13 and had just shouted at a twenty-something-year-old woman in front of her forty-something-year-old mother – and then I felt about as brave as an ant with a size forty boot coming stomping down on top of it.

But I was in for a surprise. Just as I felt myself turning back into the coward I knew I naturally was, Beth burst into hysterical tears and ran straight into the house.

"Er, I better get the dogs home," I mumbled in a panic, feeling so low I could have limboed under the broken garden gate, Precious style...

Chapter 17

FAT-TONGUED DOG, TONGUE-TIED BOY

I'd been a bit late meeting Billy this afternoon as planned, 'cause I'd had to take Rolf round the vet's first, since he ate a bee. Again.

Honestly, what kind of luck is that? Summer had been over for ages, and yet on the way home through the park from Billy's, Rolf managed to find the *very* last bee of the season to chew on. Being the very last bee of the season, it took its revenge on Rolf by stinging him before it got swallowed. The state I was in, I hadn't realized till I got home and Ivy started crying (when she saw Rolf's scarily inflated tongue) that the whole Rolf+bee-sting=allergy thing had happened. And so I'd had to rush Rolf around to the vet's for his anti-inflammatory (i.e. anti-being-an-idiot-and-eating-a-bee) jab, and then rush up here with him to meet Billy at the W3 bus stop.

Thing is, personally, I hadn't been freaked out by Rolf's horror movie-sized appendage (*The Curse of the Giant Dog's Tongue!*) – I was too traumatized by a) making Beth cry earlier today, and b) what I was about to do to poor, unsuspecting Billy this afternoon, as planned with Jen...

Omigod.

"So the reason Miss High-and-Mighty freaked out when you shouted at her was because she'd been all stressed out at keeping everything a secret from Mum and Dad," Billy babbled on, as we walked towards ... well, towards where I was taking him.

Honestly, I am so not brave. Never mind shouting at Billy's horrible sister this morning – just please don't let him notice that I'm having a panic attack over what I'm about to do to him...

"Course Mum was pretty stunned to find out that Beth had been hiding the fact that she'd got fired from her fancy job..."

I'd missed all the explaining thing back at Billy's; I'd run out of the garden and through the house with my three pooches, muttering, "Sorry! Sorry! Sorry!" to anyone who happened to be listening. Billy couldn't even run after me 'cause of the small matter of his foot still being jammed in the gate. (He was stuck there for ages, apparently – his mum only cut him free with a hacksaw once she'd calmed Beth down and heard the whole saga of what had happened in Paris.)

"Erm ... so Beth got sacked 'cause she was dating her *boss*?" I asked now, slightly hazily, as we approached Crouch End Broadway. But then maybe the stress of what I was about to do was making me so stupid I wasn't taking in what Billy was saying properly.

"Well, not so much that she was dating her *boss*," Billy grinned. "It was more that her boss's *wife* wasn't very pleased!"

"Ohhh..." I nodded, finally *getting* the whole sordid story at last.

"Anyway, thanks to you, Al, Beth can't *dare* act all superior to me ever again!" Billy snickered, looking for a second like he might stop and give me a huge hug, but then carrying on walking and offering me a high-five instead.

I smiled and slapped his hand back, knowing that some time after this afternoon I would take great, great pleasure in (accidentally) having helped to improve the quality of his life (i.e. getting his sister to lay off him for once in 13 years).

"Oh, and hey! – there's still a splinter from the gate stuck in my leg!" Billy suddenly added jubilantly, pointing down towards his combats as we (me, him and Rolf) strode on. "It's gone green and sort of septic, so that's pretty gross but cool too!"

Blee.

Still, I'd happily listen to him describing the disgusting pus oozing out of his leg, or any other drivel he wanted to talk about, just as long as he didn't do that soulful, starey, psychic thing and suss out what I had planned for him in about – eek! – fifteen seconds' time.

"Hey, you all right, pooch?" said Billy, reaching down and ruffling Rolf's scruffy head, thankfully oblivious to the turmoil I was in.

Rolf panted happily, letting his pillow-sized tongue loll out of his doggy mouth. Fat tongue or no fat tongue, he was just glad to be out of the vet's and going wherever me and Billy happened to be taking him.

"Anyway, you know the TV thing I'm doing tomorrow? Well, I can't decide if I should wear my new, baggy grey trousers, or if I should stick to my skater shorts," said Billy, straightening up and strolling by my side. "What d'you think, Ally?"

Omigod.

"Er ... I thought you already decided on your skater shorts?" I mumbled, walking purposefully along Middle Lane, towards the Broadway.

Please let this be OK, please let this be OK...

"Yeah, I know ... but my new baggy trousers are pretty cool too. Maybe they'd look better on camera. Y'know … *baggier*. And if this programme goes out on TV in the winter, then trousers would look better than shorts."

"Yeah, maybe," I said hurriedly, only half-listening to Billy's wardrobe dilemma for tomorrow's filming. All I could think about was Sandie and Billy and hoping against hope that neither of them was going to go into a massive strop 'cause of what Jen and me were going to land on them, any second now. (*Omigod*…)

Hey, anyway (I thought, trying to distract myself), who really cared about what Billy was going to be wearing? He'd be such a small, out-of-focus dot in the background that he could probably skateboard in a toga and flippers and no one watching the telly would even notice…

"OK, so I'll go with the baggy trousers. But which baseball cap should I wear?"

Omigod.

As we got closer to the café, my heart started hammering out a super-speedy salsa beat.

Omigod, omigod, omigod.

"My old Adidas baseball cap would go great with my trousers. But then my new Phat baseball cap would go better with— *Hey!* Why are we going *this* way, Al? I thought we were going to the pet shop to get that dumb doggy bowl?"

"What?" I frowned, temporarily forgetting the (fake) reason I'd given Billy for mooching along to the Broadway this afternoon.

Omigod.

"For Tor's birthday?" Billy prompted me, but trustingly (stupidly) following me anyway.

"Oh, that!" I laughed nervously. "Nah ... I changed my mind. Going to club together with my family for something else."

Actually, that bit was true. Inspired by Tor's mini-zoo of toilet-roll tube animals last night, I'd come up with (though I say so myself) a brilliant idea for a pressie, and luckily, everyone in my family happened to agree that it was brilliant. But right now my brain was melting under the strain of the secret I was keeping and I didn't have the energy to explain all about Tor's new, improved birthday presents to Billy.

"So ... where *are* we going, then?" he asked, padding along on one side of me, while Rolf padded along on the other.

Omigod, omigod, omigod, omigod, omigod.

It felt like I was taking *Billy* round the vet's now. He really wasn't going to like this. But it *was* for his own good...

"Er, I just fancy a foffy," I fumbled.

"A whatty?" he sniggered.

"I mean a *coffee*!" I corrected myself, feeling my cheeks go infrared...

The Hot Pepper Jelly café is a little bit smaller than our garden shed and a little bit bigger than Cilla the rabbit's hutch.

"Cosy!" is how my mum describes it. "Doll-size!" is what my dad says, before he starts making corny jokes about expecting to see the jelly baby family sitting at the table next to us, or pulling his knees up to his chin and whimpering on about how if he stretches both his elbows out they'll touch the walls on either side of the room.

"Hot chocolate ... hot chocolate ... hot chocolate ... and a hot chocolate!" the waitress said breezily, as she parked the four steamy mugs down in front of us.

"Thank you!" I answered, faking a bit of brightness in my own voice. (I probably sounded demented.)

"Thanks!" smiled Jen.

"..." said Sandie.

"..." said Billy.

Actually, I didn't care if Sandie and Billy were saying precisely nothing and squirming silently in their seats – I was just so thrilled that neither of them had run away in an embarrassed huff that I could have kissed them both. (Blee!)

"And one carrot cake ... one cheesecake ... and four forks to share. Is that right?"

"Yes, thank you!" I replied, just as brightly, just as fake(ly).

I was the first to take a big, nervous slurp of my hot chocolate (not coffee, *or* foffy) and nearly took the skin off the roof of my mouth.

"Eek!" I squeaked in a tiny, invisible voice. I didn't want the others to hear; Billy and Sandie would probably think I deserved some pain for forcing them into this surprise meeting.

Yep, just like me and Jen had planned yesterday, her and Sandie were already sitting in the window of the Hot Pepper Jelly café when me and Billy arrived. And, just like we'd planned, Jen was distracting Sandie with a copy of *Heat* magazine to giggle over. I, meanwhile, distracted Billy by asking him to list his baseball caps in order of preference. (I *know* – it was duller than reading the phone directory, but it least it kept him preoccupied while I tied up Rolf outside and led the way into the caff.)

"Aww, look at poor Rolfy!" Jen sighed now, pointing to his pathetic, hairy face and squashed wet nose pressing up against the glass of the window. "He wants to be in here with us!"

That wasn't *exactly* true. I could see what Rolf's

eyes were glued to, and what he *really* wanted was to have this carrot cake in his belly. If he could have got it past his fat tongue, of course.

But still, staring at my dopey dog got everyone sort of smiling, so that was a good sign.

Another good sign was that Jen had come up with this surprise forced meeting in the first place, which surely meant she cared – even just a little bit? – about Billy's feelings.

"So ... got everything packed for tomorrow, Sand?" I heard myself asking in a stupidly cheery voice. (I think I was compensating for the fact that Sandie and Billy had said nothing more than a mumbled "Hi," to each other, and only nodded their heads when me and Jen suggested drink and cake choices.)

"Mmmm," mumbled Sandie, her eyes glued to the creamy foam of her hot chocolate, and her cheeks aflame.

"Hey, Billy!" Jen took her turn, flashing me a quick, panicky stare. "Tell Sandie what you're doing tomorrow afternoon!"

Nice try. But Billy seemed about as tongue-tied as Sandie.

"Ah ... *fooooof...*" he burbled, shrugging and then tugging the brim of his cap even further down over his face.

Just as Jen stepped in to fill the silence and explain about Billy's starring bit-part in the detective programme, I spotted a disaster waiting to happen right outside. Some mum had stopped the buggy she was pushing right beside Rolf, so that her dribbling baby could "talk" to the nice doggy. Now, Rolf *is* a nice doggy, but the problem was, that dribbly baby had a biscuit in its hand. Already – as the baby reached over to pat the nice doggy – I could see Rolf starting to strain on his lead, his nose acting like a hairy Exocet missile directing him straight to that half-nibbled biscuit. In exactly one second, the baby would start wailing, the mum would assume Rolf was trying to bite her baby's hand, and next thing she'd be yelling for someone to save her child from this fat-tongued, rabid, devil dog.

"Back in a sec!" I called out to my friends, screeching my chair back and bolting out of the door.

"He's a lovely dog! Such soulful eyes!" the mum said to me, as I grabbed Rolf around the neck in what I hoped looked like a proud owner's cuddle but was actually a very firm headlock.

"I know!" I smiled frantically, using all my strength to keep Rolf at bay.

And then I saw the woman frown a bit, and shuffle off with her buggy and baby – she'd clocked the deformed tongue dangling out of Rolf's mouth

I guess, and it had understandably given her the heebie-jeebies.

"Everything all right?" asked Jen, appearing by my side and crouching down beside us.

"Yeah. Rolf hasn't had anything to eat today – apart from a bee – and I thought he was going to do something stupid there."

"Well, I brought him a bit of carrot cake," said Jen, holding out a brown sticky lump to my brown sticky lump of a dog. Rolf swallowed it before she got to the end of the word "cake". (According to the vet, he wasn't actually meant to eat anything for another couple of hours, till the anti-inflammatory injection started to work and his tongue went back to normal, but it didn't look like it had done him any harm.)

"S'pose we'd better get back inside," I mumbled reluctantly, about to cast a quick glance over Jen's shoulder at our silent friends sitting at the window table. I had an overwhelming urge to rescue Billy from an uncomfortable situation. And Sandie, of course.

"No, don't!" Jen whispered urgently through clenched teeth and a not-exactly-natural smile. "Stay here and pretend to tell me stuff about Rolf!"

"Why?" I asked, confused (and uncomfortable –

sitting on my haunches, all the blood was draining out of my thighs and my legs were going to sleep).

"I just thought it would be a good idea to give them a couple of minutes on their own – to force them into speaking to each other!"

Wow … I guess that was so smart of Jen. She was brilliant. She was going to be such a nice, kind, thoughtful girlfriend for Billy…

"So, are you going to go and watch Billy up at the park tomorrow, like you promised?" I asked her hopefully, wondering if that would be the moment Billy realized how great Jen was, and wishing I could be there to see it instead of being at Tor's stupid school thing.

"Nah, I can't," she replied, her voice still low as she scratched a grateful Rolf under the chin. "I forgot that I told my dad I'd come and watch his band play at the fête."

Drat.

Double drat.

Still, this whole Jen/Billy doodah was all trundling along in the right direction. After all, did I detect a bit of disappointment in Jen's voice there?

"Hey, before you and Billy arrived," she suddenly started to say, switching to another subject, "Sandie was showing me some photos of Jacob she took yesterday. I forgot how cute-looking he was!

No wonder Sandie ditched Billy for him! I mean, Billy's great and everything – as a mate – but Jacob... Wow!"

Cue the thunk of my heart sinking to the pavement. Poor Billy! (Even though he didn't know it...)

Well, I guess I scored zero out of ten for my match-making skills, then...

Chapter 18

KICKING BILLY WHILE HE'S DOWN

"Hey – guess who this is?" grinned Kyra, before grabbing handfuls of cheesy Wotsits out of the bowl on the coffee table and cramming them into her mouth till she looked like an orange-lipped, fat-cheeked hamster.

The other girls shook their heads and stared at Kyra as if she was barking. But *I* knew who she was supposed to be; I just didn't feel like saying anything. Anyway, I was drinking my can of Lilt.

"Hode on! Hode on!" Kyra mumfed fuzzily through a mouthful of dissolving crisps.

She reached across to the chest of drawers behind her and made a grab for a smallish baseball cap with "Alton Towers" on it. (It must have been dumped there by one of Chloe's little brothers.)

"Ge' i' *now*?" Kyra mumfed some more, with the cap perched on her curly head of hair.

"Billy! You're *Billy*!" squealed Kellie, and then everyone burst out laughing.

OK, OK ... so one of Billy's favourite party tricks

is to stuff as much food in his mouth (HobNobs/ Hula Hoops/sausage rolls; he's not fussy) in the shortest time possible. And yes, it *is* a pretty funny/gross/dumb thing to do. But Billy was still a bit of a bruised and battered boy at the moment (emotionally speaking), and it didn't seem too nice of my mates to take the mickey out of him.

It was Friday, it was about seven o'clock, and we were all in the big TV room in Chloe's humongous flat, but her mega-wide-screen telly wasn't even on, although this was officially supposed to be a Girls' Video Night.

I guess that was 'cause it was *unofficially* Sandie's leaving party, and nobody was in the mood to stick a film on and waste the last few hours we had with her. And so instead of the latest Hollywood blockbuster, the seven of us girls were concentrating more on the three Cs: crisps, chatting and crying. (Well, the crying hadn't started yet, but I guessed it probably would before this evening was over...) Oh, and fooling around, if you counted Kyra's non-hysterical impression of Billy there.

A large, colourfully patterned bowl suddenly appeared as if by magic practically under my nose, care of Sandie.

"Thanks," I said, reaching out to take a handful of black pepper kettle crisps.

"Hey! Watch out for the rat poison, Ally!" Kyra sniggered.

"Yeah, or maybe Sandie spat on those crisps!"

"*Yeeeuuuwww!*" everyone groaned at Kellie's totally gross suggestion. Even Kellie.

"I have *not* put rat poison in these crisps, *or* spat in them, because Ally is my best friend in the whole world and I completely forgive her for what she did to me this afternoon!"

That was a grinning Sandie, playing along with the joke but still sticking up for me. Though I was a bit miffed that she didn't mention Jen in the whole forgiveness bit, since she was as guilty as me for setting up the meeting with Billy in the Hot Pepper Jelly café today. Actually, it was Jen's idea in the first place, if we were going to get picky, which of course I wasn't, since it was Sandie's very last night hanging out with all of us.

"So, Sandie, just *how* cringeworthingly awful was it to look up and see Billy standing there?" Chloe grinned from the comfort of the leather beanbag she was sprawled on.

"It was *horrible*," said Sandie, pulling a face. "I felt about *that* big."

She held up the hand that wasn't clutching the black pepper crisp bowl and squished the tips of her index finger and thumb together so there wasn't even any space between them. (Wow, that was pretty small.)

"But, Sandie – after Billy went, you said you were really pleased you'd seen him and got a chance to say goodbye and stuff," Jen chipped in.

Good on Jen for pointing that out. OK, so she'd let me down by making it obvious that she'd never fancy Billy in a zillion, trillion years, but at least she had the decency to defend our getting-Billy-and-Sandie-talking-again plan.

"Yeah, that's true," Sandie nodded slowly and winced, as if she was remembering as well as I did that spine-knottingly awkward moment when we'd all come out of the Hot Pepper Jelly and Billy had tripped over his words and then Rolf's lead when he'd tried to say bye to her.

Poor Billy – any last scrap of dignity he had completely disappeared when he'd mumbled, "Well … have a good time in the bath. I mean, in *Bath*!" and then tumbled backwards over Rolf and landed splat on his skinny, not-very-padded bum. The *shame*!

"Tell us again about Billy falling over!" sniggered Chloe, which set Salma and Kellie and Kyra off. Even Jen couldn't help herself giggling. Not that he could see any of this going on (unless he was psychic – ha!), but I hoped for Billy's sake that

Sandie wouldn't join in. Ho-hum ... half-a-second of struggling to keep it in and *she* started spluttering too.

"Don't!" I moaned at them. Billy was feeling horrible enough. If he knew Sandie and all the rest of our mates were cracking up at yet *another* disaster in his life-long trail of disasters then he'd be absolutely mortified. (*Please* don't let him have bought a crystal ball recently...)

"We're only having a laugh, Ally!" Kellie smiled innocently at me. "And you know what Billy's like – he's always good for a laugh!"

"And, hey, one good thing about seeing Billy today," Chloe blurted out to Sandie, "I bet that made you realize that you'd done the right thing ... dumping him for Jacob."

"Oh, definitely!" Sandie nodded a bit too enthusiastically for my liking. "It kind of made it easier. You know; seeing how cool Jacob is and realizing Billy's lovely and everything, but he's just such a ... a..."

"Goofball!" snorted Kyra, and got everyone (except me) sniggering again.

Aaaaarrrghhh! I didn't want to ruin Sandie's leaving party, but if I didn't get out of the room right that second, I was so angry that I might have been tempted to scream, or ram whatever Wotsits were left up everyone's nose or something. I knew this was Sandie's sort of party, but did they *have* to make Billy the butt of the jokes? Couldn't they show just a *teeny* bit of sympathy for him?

How mad was this: that I was mad at my best friend, the night before she moved away for ever. Y'know, actually, for a second there – glancing around at everyone tittering and twittering – I really wished I was somewhere else, like hanging out with Billy, f'r instance. Or being fed biscuits and watching *Emmerdale* round at Grandma and Stanley's lovely flat. Or at home helping Mum and Tor make toilet-roll-tube pterodactyls or whatever for the fête tomorrow. Or helping Rowan make more of her tissue-paper roses, since she'd used her entire first batch to decorate her Johnny Depp shrine...

"Um, Ally? Phone call for you," came Chloe's mum's voice, as she pushed the door open and peered in.

"Hey, if it's Billy, ask him how his bum is!" Kyra wisecracked, as I pushed myself up off the sofa.

They were all still cackling away in the background when I got out in the hallway and grabbed the walkabout phone that Mrs Brennan was passing to me.

"Hello?" I said sharply, still irked by my heartless mates.

"Ally?"

The reception on this phone was rubbish. Linn's voice sounded all wobbly.

"What's up?" I asked my big sis, pressing the phone closer to my ear to hear her better. She'd been in charge of sorting out Tor's birthday present from us all today – was there a last-minute problem with it?

"Look, Ally, I think you'd better come home. Now."

I heard *that* all right, and didn't much like the sound of it...

Chapter 19

ERM ... WHO PUT THE LIGHTS OUT?

The walls were black, the carpet was black, the curtains were black, the bed was black, even the *air* was black. If anyone had been in the mood for a joke (and they weren't), I'd have said something about it being the perfect decor for a Goth.

But it wasn't funny. Just like it hadn't been funny when Mr Brennan – Chloe's dad – had dropped me off a few minutes ago and I'd seen the fire engine parked outside...

"It looks *awful*," I said gloomily instead, taking in the total devastation. You'd never have guessed that the walls were supposed to be raspberry. The piles of glossy magazines normally piled up and used as a table were now just a pile of cinders with the skeleton of an old lamp toppled over them. All the hand-made artworks that usually hung from the walls and the ceilings: they just didn't exist any more. The green blow-up chair was just a melted twist of dark plastic. The reams and reams of fairy lights were *never* going to twinkle again.

Rowan's room certainly didn't look like a fairy grotto any more...

"It's not *all* burnt – a lot of it's just blackened with smoke," Linn explained, like she was trying to make it better. Looking around the wrecked room, it was hard to see how it could be much *worse*. But then of course it could have.

"Thank goodness the door was closed, so the fire was contained," said Grandma, fresh from opening all the first-floor windows to air the place. Upstairs, I could hear Stanley stomping around, opening the windows in my room and Linn's. Grandma and Stanley had driven straight round here as soon as Mum had called them to tell them what had happened.

"And thank goodness for the dogs too," said Linn, leaning on the doorpost and crossing her arms. "Winslet was sleeping here at the top of the stairs, and must have started barking the minute she smelt the smoke or saw it wafting out from under the door..."

"...and of course once Winslet started, your dad said the other two joined in, so it wasn't as if anyone could exactly ignore them!" Grandma continued, opening the hall cupboard door and pulling out an old bath towel that she immediately started wafting about, sending faint whorls of greyish smoke spiralling off.

"The fire brigade were great too – they were here in just a couple of minutes," said Linn, nodding her head towards the bottom of the stairs, where I could hear the booming voices of the firemen as they chatted to Mum and Dad. (To cheer Tor and Ivy up after the drama, a lady firefighter was giving them a guided tour of the truck outside.)

"If they hadn't got here so quickly, I dread to think what might have happened to all the pets in there." Grandma stopped for a second, putting her hands on her hips and staring in the direction of Tor and Ivy's room, right next to Rowan's.

Of course. All the mice and rats and guinea pigs and fish and gerbils and stick insects: trapped in their cages and tanks, the smoke could have just sneaked right in there and suffocated them all, long before the flames got out of control. What kind of early birthday present would that have been for Tor? Losing Kevin the iguana and Mad Max the hamster and all his other furry/finny friends? Urgh...

"But how did it happen?" I asked, still trying to take it all in.

"Because of *that* thing!" said Grandma flatly, peering through her neat, gold-rimmed glasses at a soggy, blackened heap of mush in one corner of Rowan's room.

"The Johnny Depp shrine," Linn explained, spotting that I was struggling to make out what the heap of mush once was. "The fire guys reckoned Rowan must have left candles burning on it when she went out tonight with Alfie."

Double urgh … I could suddenly picture that little table piled high with photos and silk flowers and plastic doll statuettes and masses and masses of tissue-paper roses, all of it highly flammable and all of it sharing space with several fat, flickering candles.

"Where is she? Does she know yet?" I asked Linn, my stomach churning for Rowan.

"No – I tried to get her on Alfie's mobile but there was no answer so I just had to leave a messa—"

But Rowan must have got that message, 'cause we could hear her anxious voice now, calling "Mum? Dad?" as her feet pattered down the garden path and into the house, followed by another set of feet that had to belong to Alfie. After a couple of seconds' worth of hurried babbling – Mum and Dad assuring her (and now Alfie, by the sound of it) that everyone (and every pet) was all right – Ro came thundering up the stairs, her hair disentangling itself from the ornate bun she'd tied it up in tonight, her dark eyes wild with panic.

"How bad is…?"

The word "it" stuck in her throat, choking her so bad that tears started flooding down her cheeks as she stood in the doorway of the disaster zone that was once her room.

"It's OK," Linn murmured, putting her arms around Rowan before me and Grandma got a chance to. "Well, it's not exactly OK right *now*, but it will be."

As I gazed at my two sisters – one of them rigid with shock and the other one calm and kind (when you might have expected her to be angry and ranting) – I decided I'd had quite enough of this so-called holiday week. Between hassles, heart-pings!, shocks and surprises, I was exhausted.

Maybe I'd just go to bed now and set the alarm for Monday morning. I couldn't *wait* for the glorious, relaxing boredom of school…

Chapter 20

TANGLES AND TEARS...

"OK – here, we go. Ready, Ellie?"

The little girl standing in front of our (sorry, *Tor's*) stall nodded up happily at her dad.

"'*DID YOU KNOW...*'" he began reading out loud from a small, slightly crumpled piece of paper, "'*that the biggest worms in the world live in Australia and grow to more than three metres long, and you can hear them when they are crawling about under the ground?*' Hmm. So ... Ellie, how about we go and get you a lovely ice-cream? Would you like that?"

I think what the little girl called Ellie would have liked was *not* to have heard about the scary three-metre long worms. I think she'd have preferred to hear something like how many times a puppy waggles its tail when it's happy. She'd probably have nightmares about giant worms till she was 12, and never fancy visiting Australia *ever*.

What was going on here was that Tor had made his own version of a Lucky Dip. But once you'd given him your 20p and put your hand in the cardboard shoe box, you wouldn't find yourself pulling out a small toy or a sweet or whatever – you'd end up with an "Interesting Animal Fact" scribbled in Tor's best(est) handwriting.

"That little girl didn't like my fact, did she?" Tor turned and stared sorrowfully up at our mum.

"Well ... I don't know about *that*, Tor. But she *did* like the wombat her daddy bought for her!"

The toilet-roll-tube animals were going down a storm at the fête today – possibly because Ivy was doing such a great job playing with them all and getting other kids interested, and possibly because Tor was only charging 50p per cardboard pet, which all the kids milling around here could easily afford. (I just hoped that the sun would keep shining – any rain wouldn't just put a dampener on the school fête, it would also turn Tor's entire stock of cardboard pets to soggy gloop.)

"Let me have another go, please!" said a bright and breezy voice, determined to cheer Tor up. "'*DID YOU KNOW ... that when a squirrel is sad, it puts its tail over its head like an umbrella?*' Oh, *that's* an interesting fact, Tor!"

Harry was being very kind. He'd not only bought a pound's worth of Tor's Interesting Animal Facts, but he was acting like he'd never heard them before. Which was funny really, considering that yesterday teatime (before Johnny Depp and his shrine practically set the house on fire) Tor had gone next door to Harry and Michael's house and read them every single one of his facts. Harry and Michael are very good neighbours; apparently they didn't yawn or anything, Mum said.

Tor had been a bit disappointed that Michael (his hero) couldn't come today, but he'd had to work (fixing up animals – the reason he was Tor's hero). He wasn't the only one that couldn't make it; Dad was busy fixing bikes, Linn was keeping her fingers crossed for customers in the clothes shop, and Grandma was at our house, doing more airing and tidying up for us. What Tor *didn't* know was that Grandma was also making lots of food and pinning up streamers for the birthday party he was getting once the fête was over. Stanley had popped by for a little while earlier, and bought a toilet-roll-tube newt and an Interesting Fact about pygmy marmosets (they are also called "finger monkeys", apparently).

The members of the Love family who were here included me (natch), Mum (you spotted that already), Tor (doh), Ivy (our top toy demonstrator), all three dogs (with their leads tied to a stall leg to keep them from making a break for the barbecue stall) and Rowan (um...).

Wow, was Rowan down in the dumps. I'd seen Billy, Sandie and Linn all *badly* down in the dumps at various times this week, but Rowan was definitely the newest inmate of the pits of gloom. She was also my new lodger. I'd had to listen to her crying herself to sleep on the inflatable bed in my room last night, and no matter how many times I'd tried to tell her that it was OK and that no one was (too) cross with her (apart from one of the firemen, who'd made some curt comment about candles and tissue paper being – surprisingly – a bit of a fire hazard), and how no one got hurt, and how her room would be a fairy grotto again some day, Ro wouldn't come out from under the duvet and wouldn't stop crying. She was dressed all in black today, in mourning for her room, and with that combination of all-black clothes, swollen red eyes and miserable face, I bet she was frightening quite a few kids in the queue for the barbecue, where she was picking up something for our lunch just now.

"Hi, Ally!" said Jen, suddenly popping up beside me.

"Hi! Where's everyone else? I thought you'd vanished!"

All my friends had turned up, as promised, to watch Jen's dad's band play a few tunes. (All my friends except Sandie, who was doing last-minute packing today, before coming to Tor's party later, to say a proper goodbye – gulp).

When Jen's dad's band started up, I'd sneaked away from the stall to watch, and found out that a) Mr Hudson's band were pretty terrible, b) the lady ukulele player that Mr Hudson had moved in with looked like Eddie Izzard, and c) Jennifer had a middle name that she'd kept secret from us all. The truth had come out when Mr Hudson got up and said, "We're going to do an old '60s song now, and this is dedicated to my youngest daughter, since this is the song her mother and I named her after!" The song was called "Jennifer Juniper", and Jen looked like she might cringe herself into a tiny ball when everyone in the school playground turned to stare and smile at her. She said afterwards that she couldn't stand her middle name 'cause it was basically just a *tree*. I told her that it didn't sound too bad to me, considering that one of my sisters was named after a tree too. Not to mention the fact that the rest of my family is named after a loch, a plant, a hill and a building (that's me).

"We've been hanging around," Jen shrugged. "Marc from class was here – his little brother's helping run the cake stall – so we mooched about with him for a bit."

Ooh, Kellie would have liked that, since she was not-quite-in-love-but-seriously-in-*crush* with Marc...

"Anyway, we're going to head off now," Jen continued. "Thought we might go up to Ally Pally; see if we can catch a bit of Billy getting filmed. D'you fancy coming?"

Once, when I was about six, this Turkish girl called Sevgi invited me and four other people in our class to her birthday party. It wasn't just any old birthday party; it was a trip to Chessington World of Adventures, which was going to involve loads of mega rides and as many hot dogs and ice-creams as we could cram in our mouths. I was so excited I couldn't sleep or eat for a week. And then on the day we were going I woke up with measles and missed out on the whole lot. That entire day I felt like I was going to cry or die at the unfairness of it all. And weirdly – knowing that I'd promised to help mind the stall and that my friends were all off to watch Billy without me – I felt that exact same feeling well up inside me.

"I can't," I told Jen, puzzling over the hard lump of tears forming in my throat. "Mum can't manage on her own, not with the stall and Tor and Ivy and the dogs to look after..."

"Cool! See you later, then!" Jen said casually,

totally unaware of the mad wave of misery I was feeling.

Ten minutes and one burger-for-lunch later, I wasn't feeling much better, but I'd kind of figured out why I'd come over all jealous and gloomsville over nothing worth getting jealous and gloomsville over; it was just that it had been an all-round emotional week, and that emotional stuff was catching, just like the measles.

"So, how are you feeling about saying bye to Sandie this afternoon?" Mum asked, finishing her veggie burger and reading my mind. (When I say "finishing her burger", I mean she was breaking the last of it up into three pieces and feeding it to our drooling, grateful mutts.)

"OK. Sort of," I shrugged, not wanting to sound too wibbly in front of Mum when she already had one severely wibbly daughter (Rowan) to deal with today.

"Where are your other friends? Are they going to come back to the house with us to see Sandie?"

"No, they've left – they've gone to watch Billy and his mates appearing in that TV thing. Anyway, they all said bye to Sandie at Chloe's place last night, after I … er … came home."

(I said that last bit tactfully, so as not to rub in the whole fire fiasco. Luckily, Rowan hadn't heard anyway; she was chasing after Ivy, who was chasing after a small Pekinese dog that had just waddled past the stall.)

"Of course!" Mum nodded. "Billy's doing his bit-part today! Didn't *you* want to go and see him do his stuff, too?"

"Er ... yeah," I shrugged. "But I'm helping here. And then there's Tor's ... thingy."

(I said that last bit tactfully too, even though Tor was caught up demonstrating the splendour of a toilet-roll-tube aardvark to a potential customer.)

Mum pushed the sleeve of her crinkly Indian shirt back and checked her watch.

"Rowan and I could manage here for the last hour," she said, lifting up her head and smiling at me. "Why don't you dash up to Ally Pally and see what's going on? We can meet you back at the house later!"

I was just about to tell my mum that she was quite possibly the loveliest mum in the world, when an announcement came over the tannoy and Tor visibly jumped in his sneakers.

"Would all entrants for the Dog With The Most Appealing Eyes competition please make their way to the judges table now, please!"

"Oh, Ally – before you go, could you help Tor over with the pooches? Once Rowan comes back with Ivy, I'll send her over to let you go."

That was no problem. What difference would a few more minutes make? A swift trot over with the dogs and I could swiftly trot off to Ally Pally and see what was going on (I'd be even swifter if I hopped myself on to the W3 bus, of course). But – stupidly – I hadn't anticipated how hyper Winslet, Rolf and Ben would be. Maybe they'd picked up on Tor's excitement at entering them in the competition, or maybe they were just going frantic at the close proximity of all the other Dogs With Appealing Eyes hovering around, or maybe the waft from the barbecue stall was sending them demented. Whatever, they seemed determined to tangle me, Tor, themselves and their leads into one very big, very complicated hairy, barking knot in front of a bunch of sniggering judges.

"I've got one of them!" Tor called out triumphantly, as he did a dazzling bit of magic and extricated all his limbs and Ben from the tangle that was now just me, Winslet and Rolf.

"OK, you two stand back," I panted at Tor and Ben. "You don't want to get back in the middle of *this* again. And here, take this lead – see if you can pull someone else out!"

Then, as Tor pulled and Winslet began to spin around my legs in a pitter-pattering backward circle, I heard someone call out my name.

With difficulty I turned, and saw a smiling familiar someone, shyly hunching her shoulders in her pale-pink hooded top.

"Sandie!" I said with a surprised grin, at the same time shaking a section of lead from around my ankle and setting Winslet free. "What are you doing here? I thought you were busy packing!"

"Er, I'm busy leaving!" she laughed, with a laugh that looked a bit suspiciously wobbly.

"Yeah, I know, but I'll see you later at the house!" I reminded her, moving myself and Rolf away from Tor, in case – in her naturally distracted state – Sandie was tempted to mention the "P" word and accidentally spill the party beans.

"Um ... no you won't," said Sandie, shuffling awkwardly and looking anywhere but straight at me. "Mum and Dad wanted to get going earlier. They're over in the car now, with Bobbie. They drove by here so I could say ... well..."

I think what Sandie just said sunk in with Rolf quicker than it did with me. He immediately stopped bounding like a wind-up bunny and plonked his bum on the ground and let his ears sag low. You'd think he'd just found out there was a worldwide shortage of doggy biscuits. And I suddenly felt like I was perched on a bit of the world that had dropped off. It didn't matter that there were a couple of hundred (small and large) people milling around, or that there were dozens of dogs barking and whining and scratching themselves just a couple of metres behind me. All that mattered was this tiny bit of the universe where me and my best buddy in the whole of it (the universe, that is) were standing; me staring at her and her staring at the ground. All I could think of was the fact that Sandie was about to leave this very patch of universe in the next few minutes, and things in my world – in Ally's world – were never going to be the same again…

I don't know who made a move first, but all of a sudden we were hugging and crying, and I could smell the smell of the lovely coconut shampoo she always used and she could probably smell the scent of dog saliva that Rolf etc. had generously licked on to my cheeks in the last few minutes, but none of that mattered. And it didn't seem to matter that I was crying too much to talk and to tell her I was going to miss her and that I was sorry if I'd been a bit grouchy with her the past couple of weeks and I didn't understand why. I just knew that she would somehow know, just like I knew how cut up and sad she was feeling even though she was snuffling too much to talk either.

"That's my dad! Got to go!" she managed to

finally choke out, as the loud, insistent honking of a car horn parped in the distance.

And then she was gone, waving and smiling and crying and blowing her nose, and it wasn't till she'd disappeared out of the gate and out of my sight that I realized we hadn't actually said it. We hadn't said "bye". And that made me feel a tiny bit better 'cause it wasn't so horribly final somehow.

"Hu-*wooooooooooo*!" Rolf whined softly, leaning his heavy head against my leg and gazing at me with his velvet brown eyes.

"It's all right," I bent down and whispered to him, smiling as I wiped at my wet cheeks with the back of my hand. "The world hasn't run out of doggy biscuits…"

I hadn't spotted that I was now standing right beside a big, black mesh speaker. The voice booming through nearly blasted a hole in my eardrum.

"*And now for the results of the Dog With The Most Appealing Eyes competition…*"

Tor – where was he? I'd completely forgotten about him and the other mutts and this silly contest.

"*Could the winners please come up to the stage as their names are read out!*"

And then I spotted Tor, racing away through the crowds in hot pursuit of Ben (i.e. he was being *dragged* behind Ben), who seemed to be playing "tag" with a very pretty German shepherd that had somehow slipped her lead. Where was Winslet?

"So, in third place, could Bubbles come to the stage, with her owner Sangeet Singh!"

As a small, cute, brown-skinned boy and his small, cute, brown-furred dog hurtled enthusiastically up the couple of stairs to the stage, I saw one disgruntled-looking face very low down in the crowd; Winslet was reluctantly standing next to a shivery grey whippet. Maybe the whippet was always shivery, but then again, maybe the fact that Winslet – all fed up and mean – was sitting right next to the poor thing had something to do with it. I didn't know how Winslet had ended up being looked after by the shivery whippet's owner, but I decided I'd better get over there quick and rescue Winslet (or the shivery whippet, depending how you looked at it).

"And in second place, could Rolf come to the stage, with owner Tor Love!"

Er…

Suddenly I knew how it felt to be an under-study, to be hurtled into the spotlight when the star of the show loses their voice/breaks a leg/has a bad case of stage fright. Of course, all that had happened to Tor was that he'd been trying to drag Ben out from under the burger stall when his name was called. And for Tor's sake, all I felt I could do was get Rolf up there on stage, and hope Tor would come running up those stairs right behind me to proudly collect his prize (a doggy bowl with ears! Hurrah for me not getting him that for his birthday *after* all!).

But there was no sign of Tor – he was now trying to lure Ben out from under the burger stall with a burnt hot dog that the chef had given him – so guess who had to stand there like a numpty, taking the prize and shaking hands with the judges?

And oh, *boy* did I feel like a numpty. Maybe most of the audience were clapping or cooing over Rolf offering his paw to any judge who wanted to shake it, but I *distinctly* heard someone out there say, "Aww, look at that! She's crying 'cause her dog won something. *Sweet!*"

It wasn't as if I could turn around and yell into the microphone, "Actually, I'm crying 'cause my best friend left Crouch End for ever five minutes ago!" So all I could do was grit my teeth, smile, pray that I could get off this stage as fast as possible, and accept that I really *did* look like a numpty.

Ho hum...

Chapter 21

EXCUSE ME, BUT WAS THAT A PING?

It's hard to be happy when you're feeling sad.

But when it's your kid brother's eighth birthday, you've got to slap on a smile and pretend you're OK, haven't you? I hadn't quite managed it back in Tor's school playground – as soon as I got myself (and Rolf and his Appealing Eyes) off the stage and back to the stall, Mum could see I wasn't exactly brimming with joy (brimming with tears more like). Once I'd explained about Sandie's sudden hello/goodbye, she'd shooed me off home, handing me the three dogs' leads and telling me Grandma would be just the person to speak to right now.

Or not *necessarily* speak, knowing my grandma. The thing is, she's actually great to be around when you don't want to say anything. Grandma just studies you through those gold-rimmed specs of hers, instantly assesses the situation and what might be bothering you, and then shuts up, and leaves you to it, to talk or *not* to talk, depending on how you're feeling. And when I got back to the house, I didn't feel like doing anything except helping her put up all the shop-bought birthday banners and the balloons she'd just got Stanley to huff-and-puff up. Grandma gave me that look, smiled a bit, and let me get on with it. (Thank you, Grandma.)

As I silently pinned and stuck all the brilliant, multicoloured decorations around the living room, I tried to ignore the churning in my tummy and the turmoil going on in my head…

I wish that Sandie hadn't gone. (But she has.)

I wish I hadn't been so grumpy with her this week. (I don't think she even knew you were.)

I wish I'd gone up to the skate park with the others and seen how Billy had got on. (But you felt too miserable to drag yourself up there after you'd seen Sandie.)

I wish Linn wouldn't be so sad about Edinburgh. (But it's going to take a long time for her to get over the disappointment.)

I wish Rowan didn't feel so terrible about nearly burning down the house. (But it's only right that she should feel guilty after being so careless with candles.)

I wish the old, funny, dopey Billy was here to cheer me up. (But he's not around, is he? He's showing off on a skateboard in front of a telly crew and all your other mates...)

But back to the party, and back to my wobbly attempts at a smile.

"*Yaaaahhhhh!*"

Tor was so cute, he really was.

Never mind football shirts or Matrix computer games or Harry Potter DVDs or whatever other eight-year-old boys might want for their birthdays; Tor was ecstatically happy with absolutely any old rubbish, as long as it had something to do with animals.

"Look! Ha ha ha ha!"

My mini-pressie was going down a storm. Anyone else getting a small rubbery snail that spat out a long red tongue when you squeezed its shell might have thought, "Huh? Is this *it*?"

But Tor quite obviously loved his snail. Just like he loved all the other mini-pressies he was tearing his way through. (Complete mini-pressie list: a pocket guide to spiders from Grandma and Stanley; a snowstorm with a penguin in it from Rowan and Alfie; a cake in the shape of a dolphin from Mum and Dad; a drawing of something splodgy and orange from Ivy, which was apparently a "lovely deer". He hadn't got a present – mini or otherwise – from Linn yet, 'cause unlike Dad she hadn't been able to get out of work early.)

"Listen, Tor," Dad grinned, as he deftly scooped Winslet up in his arms before she snatched the rubbery snail straight out of our little brother's hands. "We've all clubbed together to get you an extra special birthday present, but we can't give it to you till Linn gets back, which should be any minute now!"

Tor looked startled, as though no reasonable eight year old could expect any more treasures for their birthday than a rubbery snail, a spider book, a dolphin-shaped cake and a crummy drawing of a "lovely deer".

"And speaking of Linn, I need to ask for a quick family meeting..."

That was Grandma. Everyone looked surprised, including Alfie (who wasn't sure if he could be considered part of the family) and Winslet (because she was a dog).

"That's right!" Stanley nodded.

He was obviously in on this need-for-a-family-meeting thing, whatever it was. Maybe Grandma was about to lecture us all on how we shouldn't leave candles burning when we went out of rooms? I hoped not – I think Rowan and the rest of us had definitely learnt that the hard way...

"It's about Linn. And Edinburgh."

You could tell by the confused/bemused expressions on Mum and Dad's faces that they were just as much in the dark about Grandma's pronouncement as the rest of us were.

"Stanley and I ... well, we've talked it over a lot. And with your permission, we'd really like to help pay for Linn to go to university in Edinburgh."

"Oh! Oh, Mum!" gasped our mum.

"But Irene, that's too much to ask of—"

"I wasn't talking to you two!" Grandma said, mock-sternly to our parents. "I'm talking to Rowan and Ally and Tor and Ivy!"

Rowan – perched on Alfie's lap on a chair dragged through from the kitchen – gave me a quick, puzzled stare. Tor didn't look any more clued-in than us, which was obvious from the distracted way he was ruffling Rolf's hair into a Mohican and frowning. Only Ivy seemed to be smiling and pleased. But maybe that was just because she'd surreptitiously stuck her finger in the icing of the dolphin cake and licked it.

"The thing is," Stanley began to explain, "between us both, your Grandma and I have a bit of savings—"

"A reasonable amount to keep us both comfortable, with a little left over," Grandma barged in and continued in her usual, practical manner. "So we can afford to help get Linn through university, but it would mean that we wouldn't be able to help any of the rest of you very much when it comes to further education. Which is why we have to ask your permission before we offer to help Linn."

Wow. You could tell Mum and Dad thought "wow" too, from the way they were opening and shutting their mouths without anything coming out. But you know something? Although what Grandma had just asked us was a very, *very* heavy question, glancing around at my sisters and brother, I could tell that the answer was easy.

"Yes, please!" grinned Ivy, bouncing up and down as if she understood the importance of the question. (At this precise time, Ivy looked like she'd be headed towards a career as an animal trainer, or maybe a circus acrobat from the amount of bouncing she did. Whichever – or neither – work or college or uni was a long, *long* bouncy way off for her.)

"Of *course* you should help Linn!" Rowan burst out. "She's the really smart one out of us lot! And anyway, *I* want to go to St Martin's School of Art here in London, so I'm OK! I don't mind staying at home!"

"And I want to be a vet, but Michael next door can teach me!" Tor blurted out.

OK, so Tor hadn't quite figured out some basic educational facts yet, but there were plenty of universities in London where he could study to be a vet. And considering his big sis would be a qualified dentist by then, I was sure she'd be happy to help him out with the occasional price of a takeaway pizza through his uni years.

"Ally?"

I looked at Grandma, and realized that I hadn't the faintest *hint* of a clue what I'd do when I left school. For half a second I panicked at the thought, and then I remembered that I was only 13 and had plenty of time to work out where or what I wanted to be in the world.

"Do it," I told her in a surprisingly commanding voice (eek!). "Linn deserves it."

"Linn deserves what?" asked Linn, appearing suddenly in the living-room doorway with a gift-wrapped mini-pressie in her hand.

"Linn's here! What's my special present!" Tor yelped, bypassing the hugely important conversation we'd just been having and hurtling himself excitedly at her. (And why not? He was only just eight, like it said on his birthday cards.)

Then as Mum reached over to grab the envelope that contained Tor's proper present (a year's sponsorship of a small-eared elephant shrew at London Zoo, with Tor's name on a plaque and everything), the doorbell rang.

"I'll get it!" I called out, though everyone else was practically deaf to it, what with the excitement of Tor's birthday surprise and the surprise they were going to land on Linn once Tor's surprise was out in the open.

I don't know who I expected to see when I opened the door; maybe Michael or Harry from next door with some animal-shaped present for Tor. But my brain had turned to such mush after a stressful week/even more stressful day that I wouldn't have batted an eyelid if Santa Claus had been standing on our "welcome!" mat scraping snow and reindeer poo off his boots.

"Hi!"

It wasn't Santa. But, unexpectedly, my stomach just flipped into a triple somersault (and landed perfectly) and a smile broke out on my face, just when I hadn't expected to feel one there for a long, long time.

"Billy!" I grinned, ridiculously glad to see him, his stupid back-to-front baseball cap, and his, er, bruised and battered body. "What's up!"

"Fell off my skateboard! Right when they were filming!" he grinned, holding his skateboard in one hand and pointing to a particularly gory, bleeding knee with the other.

I looked at the oozing knee and the vicious red scrapes on his right elbow and the bluish bruised lump throbbing on his cheekbone, right above his stupidly grinning mouth (not to mention the yuckily greenish scratches around his ankle) ... and then the strangest thing happened.

I felt almost ... *giddy*. Like I was drunk or something (though obviously I don't know what that feels like exactly, except it's meant to feel woozy and *weird*).

And then – eek! – I felt a *ping*.

I felt a ping, somewhere in the general vicinity of my heart.

Wow ... I'd just felt a heart-ping!

Urgh, urgh, urgh ... the surprises of this most surprising week weren't over yet – I was looking at this lanky, dumb, scraped, scratched and dented dork of a boy, and I realized...

(take a breath)

...I realized...

(take a breath or you'll keel over and then what'll everyone think of you)

...that all the time, the kissing dream had been about *Billy*.

Eek.

EEK!
EEK!
And the EEK!iest thing was that the dream was coming true and I was amazingly, weirdly, wonderfully moving closer to stupid, doughball, berk-brained Billy Stevenson, and he was amazingly, weirdly, wonderfully moving closer to me, like he'd dreamt the *exact* same dream.

And then (freaky or freaky!) I found myself, eyes tight closed, kissing Billy.

I, Ally Love, was (wonder of wonders!) kissing my best boy mate Billy.

And it felt ... totally eek, EEK! EEK!

(That's *good*, in case you were worried...)

Chapter 22

WITH LOVE FROM ALLY LOVE...

If you had to choose to be a month, you wouldn't pick November, would you?

I mean, it's stuck in no-man's land, right between autumn (scenic, with stuff like Halloween to brighten things up) and Christmas (snowy, sparkly, cosy etc.).

But you know, I kind of *like* November. Well, I particularly like *this* November (and I'd really liked October before it). In fact, I'd liked pretty much *every* day of the week since Sandie moved away.

No offence, Sandie – it's what happened *since* you left, not 'cause you left...

"We've missed it!" Jen shrieked in alarm.

"We haven't – this is it!" Salma reassured her, with the TV remote pointed firmly at Chloe's wide-screened telly.

And there, on BBC1, were two dull-looking guys having a secret conversation at a secret location – which just happened to be Alexandra Palace...

"Look in the background – Billy, that's *yooooo*!"

"Kyra, that's a *bush*!" Billy said wearily.

"Easy mistake to make!" Kyra grinned wickedly, while Feargal – with an even wider grin – sat by her side, making some pantomime move.

"She isn't reeling *me* in, mate!" Billy wrinkled his nose at Kyra and Feargal, recognizing Feargal's dumb attempt to mimic a fish caught on a hook before *I* did. "Anyway, your girlfriend is just gutted 'cause she didn't manage to wangle herself in front of the cameras!"

That was true. Despite Kyra's best efforts, the TV crew managed to leave Crouch End a couple of months ago without even Kyra's *shadow* slipping into the frame. She had been pretty miffed – for about five minutes, until she decided to turn her attentions from getting herself spotted to snaffling herself a new boyfriend…

"Shut up, shut up!" Chloe burst in, pointing to her hugely wide, wide-screened TV.

"Hey, it really *is* you, Billy!" Kellie squealed, her eyes fixed not on the dreary detectives meeting in secret and in focus in the foreground, but on the blurry boy flying through the air in the background.

"That was *before* you crashed, right, Billy?" asked Marc, with one of his long, skinny arms draped around Kellie's dark, smooth shoulders.

"Boo! They've changed to the next scene

already!" moaned Salma, comforting herself by taking another handful of peanuts from the bowl on the table. "I wanted to see your crash, Billy!"

"Hey, that's not very nice!" Jen frowned at her. "Billy really hurt himself that day!"

"Yeah, he really hurt himself," Chloe chipped in, opening another giant bag of nachos her dad had let her nick from his shop downstairs, "and that's the only reason Ally's going out with him – she felt sorry for him!"

"Ha, ha, ha! Very funny!" said Billy, raising his eyebrows at Chloe and making a face like he couldn't care less.

But *I* knew he cared – that's why I squeezed his hand tight, so he knew *I* knew.

You know some other stuff that I knew?

I knew that I *still* wasn't sure how it turned out that one minute – all those weeks ago, on Tor's birthday – I was standing on my doorstep, checking out Billy's scrapes and bruises and then *next* thing there was this heart-ping! and we were suddenly, amazingly, *weirdly* kissing*...

And even if I didn't know exactly *how* that happened, I knew then (as the butterflies crashed and bashed around my stomach when the kiss-thing was going on) that Mum had been totally right. You know that night – the night I couldn't sleep and Mum and me sat up watching *Dr Zhivago*, eating HobNobs and talking about love? She'd said, "One day when you're not with the other person, you realize that you miss them; that you'd rather hang out with them than *anyone* else. Then you *know* you're in love." And that was just how it was. I mean, yeah, me and Billy had *always* hung out, ever since we were little kids. But during those couple of weeks when we were together all the time, when I was trying to cheer him up after breaking up with Sandie, *everything* changed ... somehow the big dork got under my skin. When Billy was down-in-the-dumps, all I wanted was to make him happy. And when *I* was down-in-the-dumps, all I wanted was for him to show up and say something stupid and make me laugh.

Course Mum thinks it went back even *further* than that. "It's so *obvious* in all the journals you kept for me, Ally! When you re-read them, you'll see that you already were a little bit in love with him when Kyra bet you couldn't be friends with a boy. And it explains why you felt so weird – well, *jealous* – when he went out with that girl from the sports shop in Muswell Hill, and *especially* when he started going out with Sandie!"

Urgh ... why do mothers have this irritating

instinct for being right? (And why do they have to use embarrassing phrases like "in love"?)

Whatever … *luckily*, Billy felt a heart-ping! for me around about the same time as I felt a heart-ping! for *him*.

"It was when I was listening to the Red Hot Chili Peppers that day," he told me later, after finishing off what was left of Tor's birthday cake (hey, he needed his strength what with all those skate-boarding injuries). "I was listening to that and it was like wham-blam! I started pogoing around the room, 'cause it suddenly hit me that I didn't mind that much about Sandie and everything – I just *loved* hanging out with you, and I, er, really, y'know … *liked* you. All that time that you were helping me get over Sandie … I got over her *ages* before, but I just kept pretending that I was miserable about it, so you'd keep hanging out with me!"

Well, that explained a lot. Like the soulful, starey, psychic-y looks he'd been giving me – they weren't psychic-y or anything to do with Jaffa Cake appreciation like I'd once thought. They were all to do with Billy falling for me and hoping I'd fallen for him too. Which I obviously had done before I'd even realized, or I wouldn't have felt so angry with Beth for being so mean to him, with Sandie for stamping cruelly on his heart, or with Salma and

Jen for having the cheek not to be mad about him. (Which I am, officially, now. Mad about the boy, I mean.)

By the way, in case you were wondering, breaking the news to Sandie was ... *bleurgh*. At least it was bleurgh for *me*. I phoned her and let her ramble on about how great her new house was and how all right-ish her new school was, but once she mentioned Jacob and how he'd been to see her already I just jumped right in and said, "I'mgoingoutwithBilly!" in one mega-fast *splurge*.

I'd expected her to go quiet or a bit frosty or something, but instead, I heard this high-pitched screech like a double-decker bus had pulled up beside me – and then I sussed that it was Sandie squealing with happiness. (Phew.)

After that, everything felt OK. Even the teasing we got from Kyra and Chloe and the others, not to mention Hassan and Stevie and Richie/Ricardo.

"I am *so* going to tell Richie that he's a lying creep," Kyra growled now, pulling her mobile out of her pocket. "He said he ended up with a big part in this programme and he's just *such* a liar – you only saw a bit of Billy, and that was just for a second!"

"Nah, don't bother," said Feargal, grinning and grabbing the mobile out of Kyra's hand. Ha! Feargal was pretending to muck around with her, but really he was letting her know that he wasn't keen on her texting some ex-boyfriend when he – her brand-*new* boyfriend – was sitting right next to her.

Kyra had finally worn Feargal down, chasing him for weeks and weeks till he'd given in and said a weary "yes!" when she pinned him against the wall in the school corridor once the new term started and *ordered* him to go out with her. Ah, true love!

Speaking of true ... erm ... *like*; you know that weird feeling I couldn't figure out? Well, it was all down to fancying Billy, wasn't it? I've still got it, actually, but I've got used to it, even if it does feel a little bit like indigestion. It's totally different to the feeling I used to (OK, *still* sometimes) have about Alfie, which is like the silly, fluffy, lovely crush that Rowan (still) has on Johnny Depp. But that's allowed, isn't it?

Actually, you know something else? I was flicking through my journals just yesterday (and pushing Billy away when he tried to sneak a look over my shoulder) and it seemed like there's been a *lot* of new things to get used to in the last few months...

There was Mum and Dad getting back together (yay!).

There was Ivy (double yay!).

There was Grandma getting married to Stanley (and Stanley's hairy ears).

There was Linn heading off to Scotland next year (with lots of thermals, presumably).

There was the deep plum that Rowan had just finished painting her room, with a little help from Alfie (it's so dark in there now that you need a torch as well as fairy lights to find your way around).

And of course there was the fact that one of my best friends had moved away (and another one had got a bit closer).

Suddenly, I felt my knuckles crunch together painfully, but it was just Billy clumsily squeezing *my* hand this time.

"You OK?" he whispered, while all our mates were distracted by the sight of the Crouch End Clocktower looming over a detective on the telly.

"Yeah," I said softly, giving Billy a tiny secret smile.

He gave me a tiny, secret smile back. And then ruined everything by crossing his eyes.

Ah, well ... Billy Stevenson may be a berk, but he's *my* adorable berk.

Hope you don't mind, Mum, but I think I'll take a break from writing the journals for a while. I'm saving lots of stories now for Sandie, e-mailing them to her at school when I'm supposed to be working on whatever snoozeville computer project our teacher has set us.

Anyway, you're here now, and can see everything – our disasters, our ditziness, the layer of pet hair over all the furniture – close up. And I'm very, *very* pleased about that...

Hugs and purrs from me and everyone (human and furry) who happens to live in this house and love you...

Ally :c) xxx

* *Aaaaargh*! Billy HAS been looking over my shoulder and says that I have to write here that it was weird that we were kissing each other that first time, not that the *kiss* was weird or anything.

OK, so I've done that now, Billy. Satisfied?

Hey! Did you just cram *all* the Maltesers in your mouth? That is *so* not funny, you muppet!

SIGN UP NOW!

For exclusive news, competitions and further information about Karen and her books, sign up to the Karen McCombie newsletter now!

Just email

publicity@scholastic.co.uk

And don't forget to check out her website –

www.karenmccombie.com

Karen says...

"It's sheeny and shiny, furry and er, funny in places! It's everything you could want from a website and a weeny bit more..."

☆ STELLa etc. ☆

To: You
From: Stella
Subject: Stuff

Hi,

You'd think it would be cool to live by the sea with all that sun,
sand and ice cream. But, believe me, it's not such a breeze.
I miss my best mate Frankie, my terror twin brothers drive me
nuts and my mum and dad have gone daft over the country
dump, sorry, "character cottage", that we're living in. I'm bored,
and I'm fed up with being the new girl on the block.
Hey! Maybe if we hang out together we could have some fun
here. Whadya think?
Catch up with me in the rest of the *Stella Etc.* series.
I bet we'll have loads to talk about.
CU soon.
LOL

stella
XXX

PS Here's a pic of me on a bad hair day (any day actually) with
my mate Frankie. I'm the one on the right!

"Super-sweet and cool as an ice cream" *Mizz*